I0586191

The Imminent Storm

The Altered Elite Series
Book 3

D. Burgard

The Imminent Storm

Paperback ISBN: 978-0-9857582-8-8
Ebook ISBN: 978-0-9857582-7-1

Contents

1 _____ 9

2 _____ 20

3 _____ 33

4 _____ 43

5 _____ 56

6 _____ 68

7 _____ 76

8 _____ 89

9 _____ 100

10 _____ 113

11 _____ 124

12 _____ 136

13 .... _149_

14 .... _161_

15 .... _174_

Epilogue .... _182_

For the Burgard Boys,
one thru four

The Altered Elite Series

—

.

The Amber Torch
Book 1

Joined in Fire
Book 2

The Imminent Storm
Book 3

Book 4 coming soon!

dburgardbooks.com

The
Imminent
Storm

1

—

Mark's gasping breaths tell me that he's suffocating, dying . . . but all I can do is run. Run through the forest that surrounds me . . . a forest I've been in before, one I must get to again. Every fictitious step I take fills me with dread, but I keep running. Keep running because I know it's time; I've chosen, so it's time.

Being caught between this world of illusion and the urgency of reality keeps my body reactive, but it's hardly helpful.

I hear him dying, know it's possibly only a matter of seconds before he does, so I force the connection . . . then gasp, obliterating any effect the vision has on me the moment my mind makes sense of what I'm seeing.

I'm straddling him. Instinctively holding his massive frame down as his entire body violently shakes, convulsing underneath me.

The lingering smell of burnt flesh triggers the memory, reminding me of what I did to him just minutes before . . . of the horrifying implication of us taking our relationship to the next level.

I branded him. Like I've done with the others I've chosen, but this is different; he's not like them, he's human. He's not some special person who's had their DNA altered by puberty . . . irrevocably changed so as to possess special abilities— one being the ability to withstand my branding. Branding, with its internal heat and burning flesh, accompanying my selections of those lucky enough to be chosen as part of the super team.

So yes, I chose Mark, but the difference is now he's going to die.

"Please. Please don't leave me," I plead, sobbing as I continue to try and hold him down and control his unrelenting, wild movements.

The front door opens suddenly, and Sandy rushes in alarmed, given his hearing ability he's obviously picked up on the fact that things weren't right in here.

As soon as he sees us he stops, frozen in place as he stands there, shocked and staring.

"He's dying," I sob hysterically to him as Mark's gasps for air become increasingly more urgent.

It takes him a few seconds to digest the scene, to digest my words before he runs over to us. He starts to reach out, to help me hold Mark's massive frame still, but pauses, not wanting to touch his bare skin. As if doing so could somehow interfere with what obviously had been going on between Mark and I only moments before.

"Please," I plead, still sobbing.

He responds to my plea and begins helping me try to hold Mark against the bed.

"Jo, remember what you did for Gio?"

Gio. I had saved her, yes, but that was different. She was one of us.

"But he isn't—"

"Try to heal him," he says urgently, instantly breaking me from my sobbing funk.

I close my eyes and try to concentrate on my internal energy source. I think about it entering his body, then spreading throughout, healing all along the way. I picture it in my mind as I gently push on his chest.

My stomach roils in response as that familiar sweet taste instantly ignites my recollection of this one ability I possess. The one that saved Gio and now could possibly alter this tragic turn of events.

Immediately the convulsions cease, and Sandy steps back. I watch Mark's body settle, his breathing become steady again.

"You have to be okay, you just have to be," I whisper to him as tears continue to stream down my face, pelting him with the effects of my own dismay over what could have been.

I watch as his chest slowly moves up and down. A testament to the fact that he is no longer dying, that losing him forever isn't a looming ramification of having made love. Reaching out, I touch his warm face, which is thankfully not feverish or sickeningly cold.

Lingering waves of nausea mixed with my momentary elation over Mark's new prognosis are quickly pushed aside when I realize how this all must look to Sandy—Mark and I both nude with me atop his motionless body. My face wet from all my hysterical sobbing.

Self-consciously I ease off him as I hurry to grab my clothes off the floor. Thankfully Sandy turns away. I don't know why I care since he's already seen all I have to offer. Even worse, he was forced to bear witness to my undying feelings of love for the one person who constantly keeps Sandy's fateful destiny with me from becoming a reality.

"I branded him," I say, stating the obvious but wanting him to know that not only am I dressed but I'm also ready to have this conversation.

"I saw."

Just then Mark's body jerks as he lets out a raspy breath. We're both on him immediately, Sandy checking his pulse while I hold back another emotional meltdown.

"Will he be all right?" I ask, feeling the sting of my tears break through my weakened mental barrier. I gently pull at the balled-up blanket, attempting to cover him. To give him the privacy I know he'd want if he knew Sandy were standing over him checking his vitals.

Sandy and I both see it at once—blood. My heart sinks as I stare at the large, bright red stain soaked completely through on the blanket.

"Oh my god," I say right before I realize what I'm looking at. Appalled, I look at Sandy and know he's well ahead of me. It's not Mark's blood, it's mine.

"We need to get Gregor. I'll go make the call," he says abruptly, then heads out the door, leaving me mortified, wondering how I'm ever going to be able to face him again.

Seeing it sitting there, I can't help but react. Flinching, I raise my hand and stare at the skin on my palm. The red, raw flesh quickly becoming smooth again as it heals; as the amber glow melts away, fading back into the recesses of my energy source.

Chi notices but doesn't say a word. Just stands there next to me, a contemplative ally ready to protect me at a moment's notice.

She had appeared out of nowhere earlier to help Sandy deal with the twins—the girl, Reese and her brother, Levi. There they were, these two newbies to the whole team-building thing, speeding down the road, assuming they were rid of us. That they'd be able to put the entire experience behind them and go on with their lives as if those newly acquired brands resting above their hearts would end up being just a bad memory of a con that went awry. Instead, that thing that's sitting in front of me now appeared, with Chi, crushing any possibility that they would escape.

Seeing it sitting there, connected to this whole prophecy thing as a friend, not a foe, still doesn't keep its menacing aura from sending chills down my spine. Its black angular shape with equally dark windows has been too much a haunting figure in my past for me to shake so easily.

"Yeah, but it's an amazing ride," Harrison says, coming up beside me. I glance at him, standing there staring in awe at Chi's black car, and realize how quickly our interactions have become so natural. If only his brother could read my mind the way Harrison does. He'd know how I truly feel about having hurt him, having almost killed him. How losing him is something I could never bear.

"Jo, he's going to be all right," Harrison says sincerely, reassuring me instantly.

Closing my eyes, I take a deep breath, trying to focus back on the car. To this phantom-like machine that has always seemed to appear out of nowhere. Now I realize it was just Chi and her honor-bound ties to the prophecy, to me, that had her lurking in the shadows right before interjecting herself into my life at crucial moments. All because in her mind, it's her only life's purpose.

So it makes sense then that she would again appear out of nowhere, this time to aid Sandy and his apprehension of the twins, Reese and Levi. That aid had freed Sandy up to hurry back to the tiny cabin, to me. To a scene he never should have had to witness given what I am supposed to be to him.

The image flashes in my mind. I quickly push it away,

cringing when I think of Harrison. I have to remember that when it comes to my thoughts, sometimes I'm not alone.

Harrison begins to kick around the gravel with his foot, a lackadaisical attempt at seeming preoccupied. I know he feels like it's his job to comfort me, but he's worried and I don't blame him. After all, it's his brother I almost killed.

"Jo there's no way you could have known any of this would happen," he says to me suddenly. So he was in my head.

"Gregor says you can go in now," Sandy says, suddenly coming out of the front door.

I had been kicked out earlier to get fresh air. Code for "You're acting weird and it's starting to freak us all out."

It was Mark, the prophecy . . . all the burdens of being the chosen one. All of it weighing on me with its limitless repercussions.

Sandy avoids my gaze as I walk past him.

"From what I can tell, he's going to be fine," Gregor says as I enter the tiny cabin.

My throat tightens as I stare at Mark's lifeless body still lying on the bed. I swallow hard and feel the sting of my emotional breakdown dissolve back into the pit of my stomach.

"If I were in my lab, I'd be able to give you a better approximation as to the number of permanent injuries he may have as a result of the trauma to his internal organs."

"The trauma . . ."

"From your energy source, but if I had to guess, I'd say none," he says, smiling at me suddenly, as if he's the harbinger of some life-altering news.

"You see, I believe you altered his DNA."

"Altered his DNA," I repeat, hearing the words but too numb at this point to completely grasp them.

"With him being human at the time of his branding,

I can only assume his DNA was altered either through the branding but most likely through your subsequent healing of him."

"So he's healed?"

"Looks that way, but that's not all. It's incredible; he's exhibiting signs of someone who's gone through a change, as we did."

"Jo," Mark says groggily as he attempts to sit up. I go to him.

"I'm so sorry," I whisper as tears, the unequivocal proof of how I truly feel, begin to stream down my face again.

With more strength than I would have thought possible, Mark pulls my head down toward his. His lips find mine with a desperation that's overwhelming. The intensity of his kiss floods my senses, causing my body to instantly react. He pulls me tighter to him, his desire for me deepening with every passing second. He moans, and instantly the trance is broken.

I push away while Mark stares at me, panting, wanting. I glance around the room, instantly embarrassed by what just happened. Although Gregor doesn't seem to be paying any particular attention to us, I know it's just for my benefit. He was probably just as shocked by the exchange as I am now.

"Sorry, Jo," Mark says, aware of my discomfort. "I don't know what came over me."

Before I have a chance to reassure him, he's sitting up, quickly throwing his legs over the side of the bed. Halfheartedly, he grabs at the blanket as it slides off of him, exposing his nudity. Lifting his hands, he stares at them for a second before moving his gaze up his arms, as if fascinated by something going on within him.

"Son, how do you feel?" Gregor asks.

"Uh, what?" Mark says, his attention diverted as he

suddenly becomes aware of the symbol now branded onto his skin.

"His response to the sedative correlates with that of someone with abilities," Gregor whispers to me, as if not wanting to interrupt Mark's increasing wonderment at his new physical attribute.

"I administered enough to put a human his size under for hours. It's been, what, thirty minutes at the most?"

"So then, he is one of us?"

"I'm what?" Mark asks, giving us his full attention now.

"It would seem so," Gregor says, staring at Mark as if trying to come to some conclusion.

It takes me a second to find the words. It's one thing to go through the change because your body is already programed to. Destined to. But I did this to him. I made the decision for him, without his consent.

"Mark, I uh, I . . . branded you. Which I guess altered you in some—"

Oddly, I notice he's not concentrating on my words, or maybe he's just having a hard time believing what he's hearing?

"Is this how you always feel?"

"How I always feel?"

In a flash he's up and grabbing his clothes off the floor. A few seconds later he's dressed.

"Do you all always feel so, so . . . ramped up? Like you're supercharged?" he says, then grabs me in a huge bear hug.

My breath catches in my throat as his strength surprises me.

"My god, Jo, this means you aren't leaving me," he says, pushing away from me suddenly, his train of thought having switched faster than it should. It's like he's manic.

Before I have time to even acknowledge what he said,

he's bending over clutching his chest.

"Mark!"

As Gregor and I help him over to the bed, he continues to clutch at his chest, his entire body straining to breathe. His muscles constrict as he tries to force air into his lungs. Gripping the bed, his labored breathing suddenly turns to him gasping for air. With every breath, his sounds of agony mimic my feelings.

Gregor, calm and focused, injects something into Mark's arm. Within seconds his breathing begins to settle as he starts to come out of whatever it was that was happening to him.

Trembling, I take a deep breath.

"What did you give him?"

"It's just something to calm him."

It's not long before Mark's sitting up as if back to normal. The most normal he's seemed since being branded.

"So you're feeling more like your old self," Gregor asks as he calmly checks Mark's pulse.

"Yeah," Mark says, seeming slightly disappointed.

"Interesting," Gregor says as he fumbles around in his pocket, then pulls out a switchblade, opens it, and slices Mark's arm.

"What the . . ." Mark says, just as shocked as I am.

Gregor, expecting my reaction, holds up his hand as he watches the wound. A smile crosses his face as soon as the bloody line slowly begins to disappear.

"Very good," Gregor says, seemingly satisfied.

Mark's speechless as he stares at the place on his arm where just seconds ago there was a gash. I can't help but smile to myself as I remember the first time I experienced the rapid healing thing. Remembering how utterly cool it was.

"Awesome," Mark says, standing up. He begins moving his arm around.

"Mark," Gregor says in a more serious tone than I'm used to hearing from him. "You seem to be going through the same change all of us did, but in your case your body is accelerating the process."

"Sounds good; the faster the better," Mark says, reminding me of how crazy but powerful the change could make you feel sometimes.

"That may not be the case, so I'll need you to pay attention to how you feel. Your body should start to adjust and become stable as you progress through the change, but there's just no precedent for someone changing in this manner."

"Sure, sounds good," Mark says in a strained voice. He takes a few deep breaths before things seem to settle again.

"I'll check on you in a bit," Gregor says, as he heads for the cabin door. "Jo, I wouldn't leave him alone, not yet anyway."

I nod, worried.

"You branded me, Jo," he says, looking at me as if my love for him has finally registered. "You chose me."

"I did, but it's not just that—"

"Soon I'll be through this change and a hell of a lot more use to you than I've been."

"I wasn't thinking of it that way when I—"

"Jo, I know. You were just reacting. From what I noticed, it seems to be how the branding thing works."

"Yeah, I guess."

"Hey, listen," he says, pulling me to him. "You branded me because you wanted me to be a part of all this, a part of your life . . . because you love me."

I throw my arms around him, thankful that for possibly the first time in our relationship he doesn't doubt it.

As we begin to kiss each other, he quickly turns it into something much more physical.

"You know, I think we should give the sex thing another try," he mutters, barely stopping his kissing exploration of my neck.

I know part of it is his change talking, the oversexed part, but I don't care. Right now I want to. I want to forget about all the branding, the team. To take this moment in my life and make it one of those I'll never forget, but for me, in a rare, good way.

"This might not be the best time," I say, the logical part of my brain finally taking over.

He laughs at the look on my face. "I suppose that would be a little awkward if my dad walked in."

I groan inwardly as the memory of what Sandy witnessed flashes in my mind.

Mark eyes me questioningly. "What is it?"

"Sandy walked in right after I branded you. I was just so upset . . . you were dying. I guess he heard me and thought . . ."

"Oh," he says, seeming to understand the predicament exactly.

I close my eyes, hating the fact that I'm having to relive it.

Mark smiles, hugging me. "I'm sorry that happened."

"I'm just so embarrassed."

"What? No, don't be. He was probably impressed as hell by what he saw," he says and chuckles.

"You're not funny," I say, pushing him away jokingly.

"Jo, I really wouldn't worry about it. I'm sure he hasn't given it another thought," he says, but I can tell he doesn't believe it for a second. He knows how Sandy feels.

2

—

Splashing water on my face, I avoid my reflection in the mirror. The last thing I want to see are my eyes and their unsettling reminder of the expectations tethered to me in fulfilling this prophecy and, even more disturbing, of saving the world. How do you wrap your head around that kind of responsibility?

Tonight's the lunar eclipse . . . the start of it all. Tom and the others have been scrambling, trying to figure out as much about all this prophecy stuff as they can before we're thrust into it. Thrust into a battle we know nothing about but have to win.

Gripping the edge of the sink, I can feel my anxiety, like a shot of adrenaline, course through me. I've branded the final person and with that have chosen the team. What now? Are we really supposed to leave earth? Up until now every-thing has been out-of-this-world crazy, sure, but to actually leave our planet . . . ?

I yank a towel off the rack and bury my face in its soft, dry fibers. Breathing in its clean scent distracts my senses just enough that I begin to feel myself settle. Feel myself break free from all the worry. Drying my face completely, I look in the mirror and think of Guida. How she's come to guide us. If there's one thing I need right now, its guidance.

Walking out of the bathroom, I look over at the bed, expecting Mark to still be there resting, changing. He's gone.

"We don't have a choice. We leave tonight," I hear Tom say from downstairs, suddenly drawing my attention to a conversation that should be well out of my earshot.

"Okay, then, what's your plan?" I hear Mitchell say, able to tell he's being sarcastic even from all the way up here.

"The way I see it, that's your job, not mine," Tom says.

"Mine? I thought you're the self-proclaimed leader."

"Leader, but not the strategist—that's all you."

"So you're saying I'm supposed to come up with a strategy. Are you high? How the hell do I plan for something I know nothing about? I don't know the enemy, terrain—hell, not even the time frame for when this whole thing's going to go down. It's impossible."

"No, it's not impossible," I hear Harrison say then.

"Listen, kid, I know you saw something, but relying on intel from a vision is asinine."

"Maybe in the past, but—"

"No, always!"

"Hey, watch it," I hear Mark say.

"Or what afterthought?"

"That's enough," Sandy says.

"Really, you're sticking up for him," Mitchell says spitefully. "Hell, I thought you'd be pissed she picked him. I mean, you just can't seem to get rid of the guy, can you?"

"Listen asshole," I hear Mark say angrily.

In a flash, I'm down the stairs and bursting in the room.

Surprised, all the people I've branded, plus Guida, are there in the room staring at me, as if unsure how to take my sudden appearance. Even Reese and Levi, who know nothing about me, seem uncertain what to think about this crazy person just appearing suddenly.

"Jo, are you all right?" Mark asks, coming over to me. I can already see the subtle effects of his change on him. His flawless skin, the way he's carrying himself. I can tell he feels the effects, feels the vitality of being one of us.

"Yeah, I just thought—"

"We were just working on our team-building skills," Tom says, looking between Mark and Mitchell.

"Jo, I'm sorry, but my dad—"

Gregor comes over and, taking my hand, searches my face.

"It's hard to know whether your eyes are dilated or not, but your heart rate does seem elevated. Just slightly, though. Not enough to suggest a significant increase in your internal energy source."

"Probably just nerves," I say, giving Gregor a reassuring smile as I pull my hand away slowly.

"Of course," he says, seeming disinterested in my nerves.

"He's wondering how you're going to turn that big rock into a space portal without his energy-booster thing from the lab," Tom says.

He's not the only one.

"I'm sure she'll figure it out. I've always found her full of surprises," Mitchell says, eying me.

"Speaking of surprises, what about the two of you?" Tom says to Reese and Levi. "Are you full of surprises?"

Both pointedly astute, they glance around the room with the same piercing green eyes.

Tom looks at them skeptically. "I mean, you're twins, so if you're part of all this, there must be an advantage to that. I can only assume you have some sort of special twin powers or something."

"We do," Reese says, smiling, as her brother eyes her strangely. "Let's see," she says, then puts her hand on her chin as if thinking about it. "Oh yeah, how about . . . wonder twin power." She puts her fist up toward her brother. "In the form of an asshole; oh wait, you've already got one of those," she says to Tom smugly.

"You're hilarious," Tom says, smirking.

"At least that's one thing we know about her," Gio says, giving Reese a strange smile. I can't tell if she wants to rip her heart out or if she actually likes her. With Gio, you never know.

"Listen, I'm not going to be able to coax the two of you into this whole prophecy thing," Tom says, irritated. "So if I were you, I'd play along. As it is, you're going to have to pick up most things as you go."

"Nothing we're not used to," Reese throws back at him as she begins to saunter around the room.

Branded or not, Reese seems to have decided she isn't going to simulate, and if it weren't for her brother, Levi, who seems to be the more grounded and contemplative of the two, I get the feeling she'd be out the door.

I suddenly notice Levi give his sister an odd look. Before I realize what's happening, Chi has Reese pinned on the ground with one of her small spears raised above her face, poised to strike.

"You shouldn't try to take things that don't belong to you," Chi says, flashing her strikingly prominent canine teeth as she smiles at her threateningly.

With more attitude than anyone in her position should express, Reese glares at Chi as Chi starts to loosen her grip on her.

Just as I think Chi's about to let Reese go, she reacts.

With a sudden burst of speed, she stabs Reese with a series of quick jabs to three separate areas of her body. Although each of the wounds must be nonlethal, watching Reese being stabbed in such a quick, violent manner leaves me in shock.

A minute later and Chi's back on the other side of the room, leaning against the wall as if nothing had happened. As if her ability to transition from being on guard with her surroundings to actually engaged in bloodshed is as easy as changing her shirt.

As her wounds heal, Reese eyes Chi in her usual manner. Even though most people would be a little freaked out by someone stabbing them, Reese doesn't seem fazed at all. As if she could still be planning to get her hands on some of the goods tucked away inside Chi's jacket.

It doesn't take long before everyone's moved on.

As I watch the way the twins react to Tom, I'm amazed not only by their identical physical features but by the sameness of their mannerisms. The way they both look defiantly at Tom whenever he starts to get pushy, or both start fidgeting at any question pertaining to their youth or upbringing.

But even with their uncanny exactness, it's something else entirely they're doing that's hitting a nerve. They seem to be communicating with each other without speaking. Subtly interacting while those around them are completely unaware. If it were any other time in my life, I likely wouldn't notice, but not now. Not when I've gotten so used to Harrison and our own knack for talking without the use of verbal cues.

"Listen, I get it. You're orphans, raised in the system. Bouncing around from one foster home to another until, what, you started to feel things you couldn't explain, maybe even started doing things, unbelievable things. So you took off, hit the streets, surviving purely with your newfound abilities—robbing, squatting, whatever—until your abilities had progressed enough that you were able to pull off full-fledged cons. Now that must have been thrilling."

"Well, if you've got a talent, you might as well use it," Reese says, smiling smugly.

"Wow, what a couple of heroes."

"You know, we didn't ask to be part of this prophecy or whatever," she says, thoroughly miffed now.

"Yeah, that's pretty much the consensus, girlie." Mitchell smirks.

"Girlie?" Reese says, squaring her shoulders, her fists clenched in a way that tells me, as usual, Mitchell's hit a nerve. I'm starting to feel like instead of an annoying personality trait, it's actually one of his abilities.

"I've dealt with so-called 'men' like you before," Reese says, her eyes raking over his massive frame.

"I don't think so. The fact that you're still living, with a mouth like that, tells me you've never met a man like me before."

She glares at him.

"It's always about wanting to control others."

Mitchell chuckles as if enjoying the challenge. "Wanting to . . . honey, being able to control others is the reason I'm standing here right now."

"Okay, you two," Tom says, irritated. "We're running out of time."

Tom turns to Levi. "This is what I think. You're the serious, quiet one, the one who thinks before he speaks. While your sister here is, well, the one that seems to do just the opposite. So from what I can tell, and I can understand why, you're the one who calls the shots."

Reese scoffs.

"Yeah, I thought so," Tom says. "So other than your sister's authority issues, what else do you have to offer?"

"I think we'll keep that to ourselves for now."

Tom stares at Levi contemplatively for a moment, then smiles. "Okay, boss, you do that."

The moon, full and eerily red, hovers above us like a large luminous signal. Predominant against the dark sky, it sits there as if to reiterate the importance of what we're about to do. Of the prophecy we're about to begin.

We've all made it up the mountain to Mitchell's cronies, ordered to guard the cave and what's inside, now and even after we leave.

Mitchell isn't taking any chances that our only way back home might be damaged and rendered unusable, so he's leaving Joshua in charge of some tech-heavy security protocol. Some plan that includes these guys being dispersed in and around the area, armed with some sort of gadget Gregor invented and was going on and on about on our way here.

"Sir, they're here," one of the guys says into the radio.

"Okay, cool . . . I mean, right. I mean, I'll be right there," I hear Joshua say on the other end.

I glance over at the guy on the radio, and as soon as our eyes lock, he quickly looks away. Didn't he get the memo? I'm one of the good guys. Hell, I am the good guy."

"Are we ready for this?" Tom says. He sounds on edge, and he's not the only one. I let my thoughts wander for a moment; back to a simpler time. Back to when the thought of doing something like this existed only in that part of my mind that houses the incredible. Not even my imagination, but that part where the unthinkable, the actual unimaginable resides.

I enter the cave and immediately feel the meteorite's pull. Like some mythological siren, one of those crazy weirdo womanly creatures that lived out in the ocean. The ones that would call sweetly and ever so urgently for men on random passing ships to come to them, to be with them. Just to kill them in the end.

Hopefully my outcome will be different.

Stepping up to the large, dark meteorite, I pause and glance around.Everyone stares at me. Guida and the ones I've branded, those I chose to be part of this prophecy, stand there waiting. Probably wondering if what they've been told they're about to do is actually going to happen.

"It will. That is why I am here," Guida says, motioning toward the huge rock.

Reaching out, I touch its familiarly cool, smooth surface. Instinctively I react, searching my own emotional abyss for the trigger to wake this thing up, to turn it into the portal we'll need to make our way over to the other planet.

Within a matter of seconds, we're both completely glowing, me and this inanimate object that has the uncanny ability to make me reach down into my past and dredge up enough emotional baggage to wake up my abilities in such a way that amazes even me.

I grab the trigger. Feel the power source flow through me into the meteorite, commanding it to bend to my will, to come alive.

Glowing from head to toe, my eyes must really be doing something kooky because of the way my vision is beginning to alter my view of everything around me.

It's as if my surroundings, anything I'm not focusing specifically on, seems to melt into some weird haze. Like the heat waves that linger a few yards ahead while driving down the highway on a hot summer day, the ones that hover just above the road like some entrance to an alternate dimension that you're capable of seeing but can never quite get to.

I blink, briefly scanning the cave, and realize it's the contrast to my fuzzy peripheral vision that tells me my eyes have most certainly changed.

It's incredible. The sharpness of whatever I happen to focus on. The way it immediately becomes exceedingly clearer and crisper than would seem possible, as if existing in some super-charged high-definition state.

"Uh . . . anyone else seeing this?" I hear Mitchell ask.

"It's amazing," Ava chimes in.

An awareness of what they're saying suddenly connects, and I push the distraction of my changing vision away as I really stop and look at Guida, or what seems to be slowly becoming another version of her, an altered version.

As my hand continues to connect with the meteorite, pushing into it my vital energy source, she's changing, transforming right before our eyes. As if becoming something slightly less human and more . . . alien. Like a new Guida, a new Guida to us, but probably more of the normal version for her.

"A remarkable metamorphosis," Gregor says.

With the same copper skin, she's taller and thinner than before. Extremely high cheekbones frame her narrowed face and seem to set the stage for what's now her most predominant feature, her eyes.

Looking right at me and in full crazy alien mode, it's not her eyes, or any other of her newfound characteristics that's the most shocking to me, though. It's a pattern that has appeared, as if tattooed all over her body. An intricately designed pattern of brilliant color covering her skin, making her seem like more than just a humanoid from another planet, but a walking, talking piece of art.

"Cool ink," Reese says as if amazed at what she's seeing.

With my hand still touching the meteorite, still engaged in the energy transfer, I notice it's also changing. Its glow is getting much more translucent as a shimmering amber hue resonates from deep inside it.

"You're doing it, Jo," Tom says encouragingly.

I push harder until the meteorite is almost completely translucent.

"Like your famous wizard said . . . ," the new Guida says and snaps me out of my total engrossment in the rock.

"So it begins."

Famous wizard? Even with the quote, I can only think of Harrison's earlier words, a manifestation of Jo's ideal human, as I notice her physical transformation. How did she do it? How did she alter herself?

A second later and she looks right at Harrison for a moment, then turns and steps into the meteorite. Just like that and she's gone, disappeared, as if her body just disintegrated within the core of this big boulder.

Ava gasps, echoing my own sudden feelings of alarm.

"Holy crap, she's gone," Reese says in disbelief.

"Don't remove your hand," Gregor exclaims suddenly as he notices a waning in my energy contribution to the portal.

"Concentrate, Jo," Harrison says in my head, as if recognizing something in my thoughts telling me to stop all this craziness. To step away from the one thing that has shaken my faith that, although certain unfathomable things have already happened in my life, what's supposed to happen next actually could. Not in our reality. Not in any reality; never.

I do as he says and watch as the meteorite immediately responds.

"I'm afraid you'll need to continue supplying the portal with energy until we've all gone through," Gregor tells me.

"So she'll go last," Sandy asks.

"Yes, she'll have to," Gregor says, then turns to me. "Until you enter the conduit yourself, you'll need to keep the influx of energy steady."

I nod and continue pushing my energy.

"Guida just told me that each of us is to think about her. As you step into the portal, focus your thoughts on her. She will guide us to the portal on the other side," Harrison says.

"The other side, all right," Reese scoffs.

"I think she means her planet," Harrison says worriedly, as if Guida relying on him to deliver instructions this important is a lot to ask.

Tom looks around as if he can't believe what he's about to say. "Well, on that note, I guess we should get this show on the road."

"Yes, we don't know how long Jo can keep the portal open," Gregor says, causing both Mark and Sandy to look concerned for my well-being.

Chi steps forward towards the meteorite. Glancing my way, I can see she's emotionless, a master of mental strength. She's been training for this her whole life. Not just preparing her body to do the physically rigorous things no one else can, but also mentally preparing herself. Preparing for what being a part of the prophecy would mean.

Right before she walks through the portal—no qualms, no hesitation, just step through and except her fate, whatever it might be—Tom grabs her arm.

"Wait, just wait a second," he says protectively. "So you're just going to walk right in?"

She seems unfazed by his concern.

"I think I should say something before we, uh, leave," he says, glancing warily over at the meteorite.

"Listen I, uh . . . I realize we didn't sign up for this, and it all seems like a lot, but we were chosen. Jo chose each of us because we have something to offer, a part we're supposed to play in all this. But before you step into this, this giant glowing rock," he says, then takes a second to let his own words sink in. "Before we start this, just remember what this is."

Nobody says a word.

"It's saving the fucking world," he says and a second later is gone. Through the portal, as if making the decision to walk through the meteorite was the easiest thing in the world.

We all just stand there staring at the huge glowing rock that I'm continuing to push my energy into while trying to comprehend what Tom just did. That he just walked right into it.

Ava grabs Harrison's hand as Chi and Gregor step forward. Chi immediately flashes something metal that's resting on the inside of her jacket. Her way of telling Gregor she's prepared for this and has the means to protect us. Since none of us really know what we're stepping into, she's got a point.

Gregor steps back, and Chi disappears into the unknown.

Before stepping through himself, Gregor turns toward Harrison and Mark.

"I'm glad you're a part of this, both of you," he says, resting his gaze on Mark. "I know I never say it, and I should, but I love and am proud of you both, very proud."

Gregor lingers for a second, seeming to savor what could be the last time he sees his children, then turns and is gone.

Mark quickly attempts to follow his dad, but I grab him with my free hand.

"I'll be okay," Mark says quietly to me, then smiles sweetly.

Even as I continue to keep the portal open, I hold on to him. Unable to bring myself to just stand here and watch the person I love step into what could very well be oblivion.

I'm still gripping Mark's arm when Sandy just walks right past him and quickly steps through the portal. No words, not even a glance my way. Just gone, vanished.

Seeing Sandy just leave causes me to release my grip on Mark. Misreading my intentions, he smiles right before he walks through the portal himself. My heart sinks. Within a matter of seconds, I've lost both the people who in some way, shape, or form, mean the most to me.

Another few minutes, and everyone's gone but Harrison and me. All the preparing, choosing. All the things I've gone through to build this team, and now here I am, standing with Harrison, the last to take this inevitable plunge, wondering if those I've picked are all right, if they've made it to some other world safe and sound.

"They made it, Jo. We have to believe that."

He's right. All the coincidences that have led us to this moment, all the things that have happened, they have to mean something. I nod my agreement. It's just us now. Somewhere deep down, I'm not surprised.

"We'll be waiting for you," he says, trying to reassure me as he steps toward the portal. He knows that once he steps through, I won't have any encouraging glances or even a smile from someone I love to help me take that giant leap into the unknown, just me and my willpower.

"Jo, I'm not worried about you doing what you have to," he says, recognizing the insecurities in my thoughts. "You have to know that's not something I'll ever be worried about."

I do know. It's that connection that neither of us understands but feels . . . knows. "I'll see you soon," I say and smile.

He hesitates for a moment, then nods and steps into the meteorite, instantly disappearing into its core.

I'm alone, absolutely alone.

Since the beginning of all this, it would seem like it's the first time, but it's not. Not really. I've always been alone, ultimately alone in all this. After all, I'm the chosen one.

Thinking for a moment how insane that is, I take a deep breath and step in.

3

—

The instant I'm through, I feel like I'm being yanked into some high-speed world of urgency.

A barrage of stimuli comes at me at once, forcing my senses to instantly respond, to kick into overdrive. I glance around, trying to figure out everything that's going on around me. It's like nothing I've ever seen, ever experienced. It looks as if I'm traveling at supersonic speed through some light-infused tunnel. Like some multicolor Star Trek warp drive.

Surprisingly, though, I'm unreasonably unnerved. Completely calm as I attempt to digest everything I'm seeing, feeling. It's as if being here, in this situation, is somehow not only familiar but somewhere in my mind even expected.

Catching sight of my hand, then my arm, it takes me a few seconds to comprehend what's happening. My god, it's as if they're being stretched so much that they're basically see-through. How is it possible? How can my body withstand being contorted in such a way?

Staring at this unbelievable display should be too much to take. It's just not right, not normal . . . not even remotely acceptable. Even weirder still is that I'm not upset by it in the least. What I see my body doing physically doesn't seem to be affecting my mental state at all. It's as if my body, brain, everything that makes me a complete unit is oddly disconnected.

I'm being pulled in a way that goes beyond anything I've ever thought could be possible, but I feel as though I'm not being pulled at all. No, I feel as though I'm floating. Concurrently floating around, feeling as light as a feather, while at the same time watching as my body being stretched beyond belief.

Glancing up, I notice my stretching, floating body has begun to flash by intervals of perfectly positioned breaks in the streaks of light that make up the tunnel that's all around me.

I find myself suddenly able to focus on the distinct noise that's been all around me the entire time. A shrill, whining hum. Constant and pressing with its apparent need to be a part of this monumental transport. It reminds me of the sound large jetliners make as they attempt to take off and fly through the air. To fight against gravity and use the laws of physics to put some large metal object into a situation that would and did for a long time seems utterly impossible.

Is that what's happening to me now? Am I defying all that might seem possible, or at the very least plausible?

I look at my hand again and the way it's stretched out beyond recognition. The intensity of the pull and the way it seems to be morphing my body corresponds with the fact that I seem to be flashing through space. My mind just doesn't seem able to completely grasp it. Not totally. What I'm feeling doesn't have anything to do with what I'm seeing my body do. The connections aren't there, not in the way I've ever known.

I try to move one of my arms, but my body doesn't respond. I want to gain some semblance of control over my actions. To feel like a person, a real flesh-and-blood person again instead of just a mass of cells being distorted in the most disturbing way while being sucked through a long cylindrical tube, some funky space tunnel.

That's the part in all this that's so incredible. That it's really happening. I'm actually traveling through some sort of portal, through space and maybe even time, to get to some other planet, to arrive at a destination I've barely been able to bring myself to think about until now. But here I am, being pulled there.

Everything halts suddenly. The tunnel, the crazy floating feeling, everything . . . suddenly gone. I feel like myself again. All of me linked together, functioning as a whole being. In control.

I squeeze my hand, enjoying the feel of its typical reaction even as I can't take my eyes off what's now right in front of me. I've come to a stop in front of some weird psychedelic liquid panel. Its slick, semitransparent surface looks like it's made of wet glass.

I change my focus and realize I can subtly see through it. Differences in the muted colors make it almost look like the outline of what—a figure of some sort?

Suddenly there's movement, and not giving it a second thought, I step through it.

The moment I step through what I now realize is some sort of door, Mark's right in front of me, enveloping me in his large arms.

"Thank god," he mutters under his breath.

Even as my body responds to his embrace, to my new environment, I revel in the fact that we're back together again. That none of the fears I had going into this came to fruition. The fears I could never have brought myself to acknowledge if I hoped to turn the meteorite into a portal in the first place.

Glancing around, I notice we're standing on the other side of another glowing rock. Although much larger than the meteorite on earth, the cave surrounding it is similar. Other than the stream of sunlight entering the cave through a tunnel on the other end, it's almost as if I'm right back there. Back with that life-altering meteorite I've interacted with more than anyone should with a giant rock. Only I know I'm somewhere else entirely. Something about this cave, about the way I find myself instantly reacting to being here, tells me that much.

A surge of energy, painfully hot, flows through my body. I welcome it, remembering the feeling, recognizing its effect over me, the power it creates within me. The energy contained inside this meteorite is strong. Stronger than anything else I've ever felt. If it wasn't for all the pressure of completing the prophecy, I might actually be excited with the anticipation of what I'm going to be capable of doing while here.

Blinking, I try to clear a haze that's starting to cloud my vision. It doesn't help, but oddly a couple of seconds later and my vision changes completely. Instead of seeing everything through a haze, it's as if I'm looking around with a kind of laser focus. I recognize the effects to my eyesight. It's what was happening in the cave right before I left earth.

With my body surging, I know my brand is glowing; I feel it, notice the light escaping from underneath my shirt. Even so, I can't pay any attention to it, not now. Not when I suddenly notice Guida and the others on my team looking at me like I'm way more interesting than the fact that we've all just ended up on another planet after traveling through a space portal.

Harrison's in front of me then, gently touching my forehead. Causing me to feel instantly soothed as he settles the surge within me.

"We made it," Ava says excitedly, giving me a quick hug as Mark stands by her smiling a smile that tells me how happy he is to be part of all this.

"Yeah, that was . . ."

"Trippy. I know," Tom says to me as I meet Sandy's gaze.

Quickly, he looks away. So I guess traveling through space to another planet isn't enough to erase his feelings of hurt from before.

I notice then that Guida looks much like she did when she stepped into the portal, but with subtle differences. Looking closer, I see them. They're not drastically different, honestly the differences are barely noticeable, but still, they're there.

Oblivious to my arrival, Gregor is inspecting one of the cave walls.

"These carvings, they're extraordinary," he says to Guida. "What are they?"

"Those are that which I have seen."

"Visions," Harrison mutters under his breath.

"It's us," Tom says amazedly, having begun to check out the walls for himself.

"It's the prophecy from my vision . . . from Jo's birth," Guida says as Tom and Mitchell silently study each drawing.

I notice then the entire cave is covered with the intricate carvings. It would have taken her years to do this.

"If these are the prophecy, I think I'd like to know what this one's about," Reese asks, referring to a carving in the stone depicting a planet exploding and sending debris flying out from it in all directions.

"That's the original planet. The one for which all beings like us draw our abilities," Guida says, bringing our attention to a section of a wall depicting various scenes, all etched in the stone, all beautifully detailed.

"It's going to be destroyed?"

"It already has, long before now."

"What? It was destroyed," I say in disbelief.

"We draw our abilities from some planet that's no longer around," Reese asks glancing at her brother like the whole thing is absurd.

"Of course, it makes sense," Gregor says as if coming to some grand conclusion about the markings in the stone.

"The energy found in the meteorite that fell to earth years ago, and in that meteorite there . . . ," he says, referring to the even larger one we just walked through. "The same energy that Jo can control . . . it must have existed at the core of this original planet."

Guida nods, then smiles at him as if she isn't surprised that he would be able to figure that out from her etchings.

"Right," he continues. "So when this planet was destroyed, fragments of the energy resting at its core were dispersed throughout space."

"In the form of shooting chunks of planet," Tom says.

"Meteoroids, exactly . . . but I wonder what caused the destruction of the planet to begin with," Gregor asks, thoroughly engrossed. "I would think an issue within the stability of its core or possibly an exploding nearby star."

"Or General Zod," Tom says sarcastically.

Gregor ignores him completely, still enamored by the scenes on the wall in front of him.

"So that's what started it all," Sandy says.

"Started what?" Levi asks as if trying to wrap his head around all the information coming at him.

"The maturation of abilities," Gregor says as if remembering Levi and his sister are new to all this. "Through my research we found that certain individuals have mechanisms within their DNA that, when they come into contact with the energy source found in these types of meteorites, develop abilities. So this planet being destroyed and sending its energy throughout the universes could alter many other life forms. Thus starting the very reason why we're here."

"You mean the prophecy."

"Exactly."

"What's the deal with the eyes?" Reese asks, pointing to a carved rendition of eyes like mine and Guida's.

Guida glances at Harrison.

"The ones with eyes like that are more," Harrison says.

"More?" Tom asks.

"They have more abilities or are special in some way. I don't really know," Harrison says, looking confused.

"There are certain individuals who manifest the energy differently. That we've known, but the eyes . . . so they're part of it," Gregor says as if trying to wrap his mind around what it could mean.

"Yes, the distinguishing eyes are," Guida says.

"Any chance these pretty little drawings could be bullshit?" Mitchell asks as he scans the wall.

"I wouldn't think so. Why?" Tom asks.

"Because if they aren't, then it looks like we're going to be fighting that guy," Mitchell says, showing Tom a specific spot on the wall.

"What the hell?"

"Exactly," Mitchell says.

"You saw this in a vision?" Sandy asks Guida as he gets a closer look at the impression in the stone wall.

Guida nods.

"Well, I think there's something special about the depiction of him standing among the corpses. It really seems to set the scene," Reese says nonchalantly.

"You know, whatever," Tom says shrugging it off. "I'm not worried. We have skills."

"Yeah well, it looks like he's got the eyes, shit for brains. So I'm guessing he's got skills, too."

"Damn," Tom mutters under his breath as he studies the wall for a moment longer.

"How do we fight someone like that?" I ask, staring at the carved rendition of someone I have a feeling is going to be haunting me for the rest of my life. That is, if I have a life after dealing with him.

"We prepare," Mitchell says matter-of-factly, then looks right at me. "And we hope that you live up to all the hype."

"Yes, your preparation will be the key for the lock," Guida says suddenly, disrupting Mitchell's masterful ability to dredge up every single one of my insecurities with just a simple remark.

"You mean our preparation is key," Tom says.

"Yes," Guida says, smiling.

"That I figured. What we need to know now is how we're going to be able to prepare," Mitchell says, thankfully taking his focus off me.

"You misinterpret my meaning of your preparation."

"I do," Mitchell asks as if not following her.

"You prepare in terms of strategy, plans. That is why you were chosen."

"I was chosen because I know how to plan," Mitchell asks.

"Yes, because of the way you think," she says, and I notice then that her appearance has subtly changed yet again from what it was even a few minutes ago. So minor it's barely noticeable, but still . . .

"Okay, so I take it that's not what you mean when you say prepare," Tom interjects, as if getting frustrated by the circular conversation.

"It's the preparation of your abilities. That's the key that will unlock that which will make you more than saviors of my planet and your own."

"More?"

"Yes, you are all to be more than the prophecy," Guida

says, then abruptly turns and heads toward another area of the cave.

Tom swears under his breath as Mitchell stares after her.

As a thousand questions pop in my mind, I can't help but push them away. It's hard enough to focus on the monumental task fate has assigned me now. How could I ever wrap my mind around some other unspoken act of heroism that I may be destined for down the road? I can't. Not when I don't even know if I'm up for this one.

"Now we must leave here," Guida says, picking up a strange metal boomerang-looking thing.

"Where are we going?" Tom asks.

"To the place where it will begin," Guida says, offering the strange object to Gregor.

"What place? What have you seen," Mitchell asks looking irritated.

Ignoring him she watches Gregor with an amused expression.

"I've never seen metal like this. What are its properties?" Gregor asks as he studies the object.

"Is it a weapon?"

"If that's a weapon, then I'd say there's not going to be much out there to fight," Reese scoffs.

Guida smiles at her. "Do not use its cover to gauge the book."

Reese looks at her quizzically.

"On this planet, those who wish not to fight sometimes must, just as those things that may seem harmless aren't," Guida says, then turns and heads toward the exit without another word.

"Great, that makes feel better about all this," Tom says sarcastically.

Apprehensive as we make our way through a long narrow

passageway toward the light, I can't help but feel the energy within me come alive. Like some friendly reminder of my role on all this, of the expectations.

Chi, positioning herself between me and anything we may encounter once we leave the security of this cave, seems satisfied that Mark and Sandy, ever vigilant as well, stand on either side of me.

I thought I was the chosen one . . . the one in control of the ever-powerful energy source. Why am I the one always being protected?

Mitchell, his usual dark dominance setting in, instantly changes my perspective as he reminds everyone of the importance of keeping me alive. Not to fulfill the prophecy, nor out of any true concern for me. No, it's because I'm the only one able to open the portal, thus I'm the only one who can get him back home when it's all said and done.

At least I can always count on him to keep me grounded in all this.

A minute later and we're stepping outside on an alien world.

4

—

eaving the cave we find ourselves in the middle of a
lush green forest. On edge, everyone takes in their surroundings. Tall trees envelop the entire area, providing
a protective canopy for a wide array of dense vegetation. As
I glance around, I can't help but be amazed at how familiar
and typical it all seems. How can it be that we find ourselves
on another planet that has such similar plant life to that of
Earth?

"They're the perfect luminosity to sustain life . . . everything our scientists said could be possible. It's incredible,"
Gregor says to no one in particular as he gazes at the sky.

Looking up, I'm shocked by what I see. It didn't seem
real when we were still in the cave next to the portal, or even
as we stepped outside into the surrounding forest, but as I
scan this horizon, the enormity of it sinks in.

This planet has two suns, which in itself should be odd
enough, but it's what's off to the right that makes me feel like
I'm looking at the cover of one of those crazy science-fiction
novels. Pale gray with tan splotches, it's a massive planet.
Dwarfing the two suns, it just seems way too large to be hovering so close to us.

It's hard enough just to wrap my head around the fact
that we're on another planet, but even more unbelievable . . .
the fact that we're on another planet in a completely different
universe.

Sandy mouths something to Gio, causing her to nod
then, give him a reassuring smile. Well, at least they seem

back to normal—friends, partners, whatever; more than I could ever hope to be after what I've put him through.

"The smaller sun seems to have a much higher metallicity than the larger one. Like a little brother with all the talent but relying on the bigger brother for emotional security," Gregor says, smiling to himself.

"What do you mean?"

"Oh, well, you see," Gregor says, realizing that people are actually interested in his observations, "the more red a sun is, like that one"—he says pointing toward one of the suns—"the more metals it has, which means the more likely the star system is to have gas giant planets . . . like that one." This time he points to the huge gray planet.

"Having two suns can also affect weather," Levi says, surprising everyone.

"Yeah, my brother's kind of a science geek, too. Especially when it comes to storms," Reese says, then seems sorry to have said it after Levi gives her a strange look.

"You're right," Gregor says, seeming impressed with him. "Having two suns can cause a variety of cosmic ramifications . . . especially in regards to weather."

"What do you mean 'ramifications,'" Mitchell asks, his interest piqued with the mention of weather.

"It's hard to know exactly. It's not just two suns that can cause cosmic weather but also the positioning of planets."

"Cosmic weather," Tom says, irritated. "What the hell's that?"

"Hypothetically speaking, we're talking solar wind, storms, tornados."

"Doesn't sound any different than the weather I've dealt with before," Mitchell says as if it's one less thing he has to worry about.

"Sometimes it isn't, but solar wind can be strong,

conceivably stronger than the wind from any tornado we've ever heard of. But most likely, that won't be the only problem," Gregor says.

"What do you mean?"

"You see the wind can also speed up particles in the atmosphere, which then would increase the amount of lightning strikes."

"Okay, so more lightning."

Levi chimes in then. "We're not talking about just any lightning."

"How would you know?" Tom asks, still trying to figure out this new brother-sister duo.

"I read," Levi says smugly. "Plus, I've always had an interest in lightning."

"You have, huh?"

"Yes, I have," Levi says. "You see, we're talking dry lightning, possibly even superbolts."

"Superbolts?"

"Yeah, the most intense lightning strike you could ever imagine. No rain, no thunder . . . just a flow of current hitting you without warning."

"Superbolts . . . now, that sounds fun," I hear Reese whisper slowly in her brother's ear as she leans in, lingering closer than she should. What is it with these two?

"We should not stay in one place long," Guida says, seeming uncharacteristically uneasy.

"What, why?" Tom asks as we all begin to follow her as she makes her way through the trees.

Mitchell, eying Chi and Sandy, scans the area around us as if trying to get a sense of it. He's not stupid. This place may look a lot like any number of forests back home, but he, probably more than the rest of us, knows it's not.

"Jo, you ok?" Mark asks me, as if noticing my nervousness.

I nod and try to smile reassuringly, but as we walk along, I can feel the energy within me.

"Incredible, huh?" Mark says softly to me, then glances up at the foreign sky as if trying to distract me.

It works. I remember then that, surprisingly, I haven't noticed him having any more effects from his change since we came to this planet.

"So how are you doing with everything? I mean, are you feeling okay?" I whisper to him.

"I'm feeling way better than okay," he whispers, smiling enthusiastically before getting serious.

"Honestly, Jo, I've never felt like this before. I mean whoever's coming, whatever it is we're going to have to fight, at least I know I'll be able to help this time."

"You've always been able to help," I whisper, reaching out and touching his hand reassuringly as we walk along.

"Yeah, well, I don't know about that."

I notice Guida looking at me quizzically, as if she still can't make sense of my attachment to Mark. It's when I see Sandy watching our interaction that I realize why. She's probably reading our thoughts, and to her, Sandy's my soul mate or whatever, and I guess in her world, that means more than I could ever understand.

"So in this type of volatile environment, where do you live?" Gregor asks Guida, as if the question just popped in his head.

"There," she says, pointing to a large rock-like structure far off in the distance.

"Everyone on this planet is there," Harrison explains for Guida.

"Every single person, uh . . . or person like you, is in that one place?" Tom asks.

Guida nods, seeming apprehensive about our surroundings all of a sudden.

The others notice it, too, which only adds to everyone's uneasiness.

Mitchell mutters something under his breath, and as if understanding his concerned grumblings, Chi, Sandy, and Gio move to the edges of our entourage.

Before I even realize what I'm hearing, I feel my body react. Feel the stinging of my palms, telling me that the energy source somewhere deep within me is quickly becoming more accessible.

"Jo, what is it?" Mark asks.

I can't answer. Can't bring myself to, as I suddenly realize what I'm hearing . . . a low, eerily deep growl coming from somewhere deep in the forest. I try to focus on the sound, but within seconds am distracted when the dense foliage to the right of us begins to move.

Ava gasps just as Mark takes a protective stance between me and whatever is in those trees.

"Uh, Guida, should we be concerned by this?" Tom asks, not taking his eyes off the rustling limbs.

Chi and Mitchell suddenly brandish weapons, leaving me hopeful that they may have prepared somewhat for this whole prophecy thing, or at the very least that they're able to protect us from whatever is making its way closer.

As the rustling grows stronger, Chi steps in front of me with one of her small spears in each hand. Suddenly, spilling out of the trees and into view are a dozen or so of the cutest little furry animals I've ever seen.

Lifting themselves up on their small hind legs a few feet away from us, they stop and stare at us with their round, dark eyes.

"You've got to be kidding me," Tom says, causing all the little animals to look right at him simultaneously.

Although momentarily relieved, I feel my body surge

slightly. I know I heard something else out in the forest. Not something that could have come from small, cuddly creatures. No, it was completely different . . . it was threatening . . . frightening.

"They're so sweet," Ava says, walking over to one of the fuzzy little creatures as Harrison tries to stop her.

"Honey, I wouldn't do that," Mitchell says, warning her.

Tom and Sandy, both alarmed, in unison say, "Don't—"

"They're so soft," Ava exclaims as a few of them surround her, letting her pet them.

Guida seems unsure what to think as she watches their interaction with Ava. Sandy and Tom, noticing Guida's reaction to the display, try to get Ava to come away from the animals.

"It's okay, they like me," Ava says as she sits on the ground, giggling as they jump in and out of her lap and all around her. Even though they seem to be warming up to her quickly, they still eye the rest of us skeptically.

As if unable to resist the charms of Ava's furry friends, Reese and Gio head toward them, but as soon as they get close, the little animals playfully keep themselves just out of their reach.

"Josephine, it seems you're not the only chosen one," Gio says sarcastically as the animals continue to move away from her while still wanting to be around Ava.

"Jo, Guida seems weird about this. I'm not used to her, well, her thoughts feeling like this," Harrison says worriedly to me alone.

Concerned by his words, I start to head toward Ava and the little creatures myself, but Mark and Sandy aren't having it. Instinctively, they both reach out to stop me at the same time.

That's when I sense it . . . movement, a sound maybe. Something far off in the forest. No one else seems aware, so

I start to think I'm just imagining things until I watch the little animals freeze as if they themselves hear something. A second later and they take off, back into surrounding trees.

"You see that?" Mitchell says, bringing our attention to the fact that the rustling foliage is happening all around us. "They're smart, and were surrounding us the entire time. Probably hundreds of those things, sitting out there watching as their friends interacted with us."

"Holy hell," Tom mutters under his breath as he glances around.

Ava, the only one who doesn't seem a little freaked out by Mitchell's observation, says, "They just wanted to get to know us; they wouldn't have hurt us."

"Maybe they wouldn't have hurt you . . . The rest of us, who knows?" Tom says.

I suddenly realize something is headed right for us. It's huge and moving fast. Even from this distance, I can hear the tree limbs snap under its weight.

"There's something's coming toward us," I yell, feeling my body surge the moment I hear its snarling, labored breath.

Before any of us has a chance to conceive what's happening, something large, still far enough away to stay out of sight, blasts through the trees to the side of us, then keeps going until I'm unable to hear it again.

"Fuck me! What the hell was that?" Tom exclaims.

"Guess we know why our little friends left so quickly," Mitchell says, looking spooked.

Still surging, I begin to feel my body ramp up even more. Just when I start to think I'm going to begin shooting energy bursts out of my pores or something, Harrison's beside me, swiftly calming me down with just his usual touch.

"We have to go," he says, as Guida quickly starts walking toward her large rock home.

"I'm with the alien lady," Reese says, motioning for Levi to come with her.

We move quickly through the forest. With Chi and Mitchell in the front and Sandy and Gio bringing up the rear, no one says a word as we all try to digest what just happened. This forest may look familiar to us, like we're on our own planet, but that thing lurking deep in the woods; it's quickly reminded us we're not.

As we all walk along, I try to wrap my head around the monstrous thing that's out there. How could something be that seemingly large and heavy but still move so fast?

Coming up beside Mark and me, Sandy's all business as he says, "Jo, you'll hear something before the rest of us."

I nod, knowing what he's getting at: knowing that there's a good chance that thing will come back.

Listening intently, I'm on edge, but thanks to Harrison, not surging as we move along at a steady pace. Occasionally I notice a few clusters of delicate, beautifully colored purple flowers among the green, sturdy vegetation and wonder how strange it is to see something so fragile growing here.

I pluck one from a grouping. Gently I run my fingers over its soft petals and notice some of its rich purple color coming off onto my hand.

Reese, as if the unusually placed flowers aren't lost on her, either, grabs one as she walks by, breathing in its scent while Ava, also seemingly enthralled by the purple beauties, embellishes her golden hair by placing one of them behind her ear.

"On this planet, you must always be cautious . . . even of its beauty," Guida says, looking uneasy at the pretty flowers.

Quickly I rub my hand on my pants just as Ava grabs the flower from behind her ear and tosses it to the ground. They look like they're just flowers, but the way Guida is avoiding them as we walk by tells me they must be more than that.

Taking a moment, I pay special attention to my surroundings but don't hear anything. At least nothing that would make me think that the monster, or whatever it is, is anywhere around us.

"Do you hear it?" Mark asks quietly.

Looking at him, I shake my head in response, then find myself lingering over his eyes, then down to his lips . . . those lips, so perfect, so kissable. How I wish we were back at that cabin again.

"Jo," he says, looking at me as if confused by my gaze.

Embarrassed, I look toward Harrison, wondering if he was listening. Where the heck did those thoughts come from?

Smiling, I watch as Ava gives Harrison some flirty looks. They are just so darn cute, I think to myself right before a dizzy spell comes and goes so fast I begin to wonder if I imagined it.

That was bizarre.

"Are you okay?" Harrison asks me, looking worried but not wanting to alarm the others.

"Not really, no. I can't hear it growling anymore, can't hear it moving. How do I keep Sandy from getting hurt? I mean, I want Mark . . . I need him," I say, then am quickly horrified when I realize I said it out loud.

Why would I say all that? What's wrong with me?

"Jo, what are you talking about?" I hear Mark ask as he walks along next to me. I don't answer him; I can't. I'm too busy getting through another dizzy spell.

I notice Ava then, smiling as if on a date, not walking through creepy alien woods, suddenly grab Harrison's hand in her own. Although he seems surprised, it isn't until she brings it to her lips and starts kissing it that he looks toward Mark as if unable to understand this abrupt display of affection.

Reese, as if also on board the crazy train, links her arm in her brother's. Pulling him toward her, she whispers something in his ear. Visibly flustered by whatever she said, he gently pushes her away.

What's going on? Why are Ava and Reese acting so weird? Why am I acting so weird?

With my thoughts preoccupied by another strange dizzy spell, I barely notice that the sporadically placed flowers have grown in numbers. We're surrounded by them, by the beauty of their deep purple hue.

As everyone avoids touching them, I glance over and catch sight of Gio staring at Mark in a way that instantly makes me wish I had one of Chi's discs. Why does she always have to check him out . . . always have to rake her eyes over his body like that? The same body that's burned into my memory from our time together in the cabin. When his large, naked body frightened me with his need of something I had to have. The same thing I find myself wanting to have right now.

"Uh, Jo," I hear Harrison say in my head, just as another wave of dizziness rolls over me.

Leaving Sandy's side, Gio comes over to Mark and me.

"What the hell do you want?" I blurt out, surprising her and Mark.

"Josephine, is everything all right?" Gio asks, eying me strangely before glancing at Mark in her usual seductive manner.

I seethe, furious at her relentlessness to acquire his affections.

"If I were you, I'd get away from him," I say, feeling my body respond as I mentally grab her.

I want her to leave him alone, to never come near him again.

Extremely dizzy now, I hear Harrison yell something just as my vision blurs completely. Disoriented, I hit the ground, then feel someone press on my forehead.

All I can do is lie here as the world whirls around me. Minutes later and I hear his muffled voice in my head as the dizziness finally begins to dissipate. Why does he sound like that?

Slowly, I'm able to see again as my mind clears. I feel as though I'm waking up from some strange dream. A dream that's quickly beginning to feel more like a nightmare as I lie here beginning to remember bits and pieces of some of the things I hope I didn't actually say.

"Are you okay?" Mark asks worriedly on the ground beside me.

Harrison, sitting on my other side, has his head down as if he just got the wind knocked out of him. Sitting up I notice Gio's also on the ground, trying to sit up.

Mark helps me to my feet. The minute I stand up, I feel more like myself. As if just the act is enough to release the remnants of the weird mind fog.

With my mind clear again, I suddenly remember. Concentrating, I listen to the area around us. Thankfully I don't hear anything. At least nothing that would make me think we're in danger of being attacked by that thing in the woods. I'm surprised, though. I mean, if it were smart, now would be the time.

"Your nose," Mark says, suddenly noticing Harrison's nose is bleeding.

"What happened?" I ask him, more about his nose than anything.

"I don't know. Something caused you to—"

"I gave you a bloody nose?"

"No, you . . . uh . . . I had to stop you from . . . "

"Killing me," Gio says as Sandy helps her slowly get to her feet.

"What?" I ask trying to wrap my mind around all the chaos I was able to cause in a matter of minutes.

"You locked Gio in your mind death-grip like before," Tom states, as if considering it an attribute of mine instead of what it actually is: an all-too-easy way for me to end someone's life with just my thoughts.

I think back to the mission. Back to that horrible time when I almost killed everyone by putting them in that same death grip.

"As usual, you're full of surprises, Josephine," Gio says, still somewhat out of breath. "I've had plenty of women want to kill me because of their man, but you're the first one to actually try."

"Oh god, I'm so sorry," I say, knowing I should be completely mortified by what I tried to do to her but honestly not really feeling it. I can't help it; after all, she's Gio.

"I can't say I'm glad to see you still have that in your skill set," Mitchell says, probably thinking back as well on our time spent at the mission.

"Yeah, but did you see what Harrison did," Tom says, as if still taking stock of everything that went on, of everyone's abilities.

"He was able to stop her. I knew they were linked, but . . ."

"But what caused all the bullshit craziness to begin with?" Reese asks, more docile than usual with her brother sitting on the ground next to her. She looks like she's still trying to come out of the same funk I was in.

"It was these," Gregor says, using a stick to check out one of the purple flowers as Guida nods.

"It's just a flower. How could it cause us to act so strange?"

Ava says, looking a little peaked as she sits next to Harrison, helping him with his bloody nose.

"It must be a contagion of some sort. By the effects, I'd say it reacted with your endocrine system when you touched it."

"My what?"

"Your hormones," Gregor says, still checking out the flower, as if it's the most amazing thing he's seen yet.

"Hormones?" Tom asks incredulously. "Like the girly ones?"

"Quite the opposite, actually. By their reactions, I'd say it spiked their testosterone levels. That would explain their heightened feelings of aggression and sexual urges."

Sandy looks at the ground.

"It would also explain the dizziness and fainting," Levi says.

"Exactly. I'd even say with levels high enough, the contagion in this pretty little thing"—Gregor uses the end of his shirtsleeve to pick one of the little purple flowers and hold it up to the light of the suns—"could possibly cause death."

Tom turns to Guida.

"Super bolts of lightning, some ferocious beast stalking us, and now killer flowers . . . Forget the prophecy—I don't know if we're going to survive your planet."

5

—

"THIS IS LIKE THE WIZARD OF OZ," Ava says, smiling at Sandy as if trying to lighten the mood.

"Then I guess that would make Harrison Toto," Tom says, laughing.

"And you one of the flying monkeys," Reese quips back.

Walking along, we all smile at the exchange, feeling a moment's reprieve from our predicament. Having gotten close to the giant structure that houses Guida and the others on this planet, we thankfully haven't had any more incidents. I haven't heard a peep from that thing that was lurking in the woods, and the purple flowers, so abundant in the one part of the forest, are basically nonexistent now.

Since leaving the portal cave with all the prophecy markings, we've passed a multitude of other caves and boulders scattered around the forest. Although most seem to be characteristic of the typical topography for this planet, some are actually other meteorites, which caused Gregor to conclude that this planet must have been much closer than earth to where the original planet was before it was destroyed.

"You said a few of the caves that contain meteorites serve different functions for you. Does the potency of the energy source within each one play a part in determining your use of them?" Gregor asks Guida, his interest in this planet never seeming to let up.

"You always know more than you realize," Guida answers.

"Isn't that the truth?" Tom says.

"What I'd like to know is what happens in the one

Harrison called the mating cave," Reese asks obnoxiously, giving her brother an insinuating look.

"It's not actually called that," Harrison says, looking toward Guida, embarrassed. "It's just kind of hard to explain."

"So you're saying there's no actual mating going on in there," Reese says snidely.

"Classy," Gio says sarcastically.

Reese gives her a dirty look.

"I guess that probably isn't the right word to describe it," Harrison says.

"Okay. Well then, what's it used for?"

Guida seems intrigued by Reese. "You try and simplify what doesn't come simply for you."

"That's her way of saying you're a little too into your brother," Mitchell says, smirking.

"Ignore him," I say, hating his bullying ways.

"Well my interest is peaked now, so what may I ask is it used for?" Gio asks.

Harrison glances at Guida, as if unsure how to explain it.

"Guida uses the energy of the meteorite in that cave to help with, um, reproduction-type things."

"Reproduction-type things?"

"I guess you could call it that. They look at reproduction and all that stuff differently than we do."

"And all that stuff," Reese says smiling at him. "Aren't you cute?"

Harrison walks along as if unable to gather his thoughts. I sometimes forget how much more he has to do than the rest of us. I mean just being in my head would be a full-time job, but to be in an alien's, too; an alien who obviously relies on him to get her alien thoughts across. It's crazy.

"It's kind of hard to explain. I mean, they do, uh . . ."

"Procreate?" Gregor asks.

"Yeah, that," Harrison says, blushing, reminding me again that he's only fifteen. "It's just different or maybe separate, uh, from how they experience other things together."

"Well, that clears it up," Tom says sarcastically.

"Sorry."

"Don't sweat it. In regards to that subject, things get lost in translation all the time, even on our planet. You're trying to explain it about a whole other species from a whole other planet."

"Interstellar inhabitants," Gregor interjects.

"Whatever."

"So with all these meteorites scattered around this place, could that be why it's going to be attacked?" Mitchell asks, obviously contemplating more than the beings on this world and their habits.

"It's feasible. That could mean this planet could have massive amounts of the energy source."

"Even so, how would they get it? It's in the rocks, and no offense," Tom says to Guida, "but this place doesn't seem too habitable."

"There are ways to draw energy from rocks. With the appropriate equipment, they may very well be able to extrapolate the meteorite's energy source. If they're able to amass enough of the energy source, the ramifications of what they'd be able to do are concerning to say the least. The weapons they could create could be catastrophic to other planets."

"Maybe they're coming for Jo . . . I mean, she is a walking, talking energy source."

Everyone's quiet as I digest his words. Could all this be because of me?

"That's the cave we were talking about earlier," Harrison says suddenly as we walk by a cave with an extremely small opening. It's hard to believe Guida or any beings like her would have thought to ever go in there, much less use it for anything.

"That's the mating cave you were blabbing about," Mitchell scoffs.

"You, too, use a cover to gauge a book," Guida says, eying him.

"The meteorite with the strongest energy on this whole planet is lying inside there," Harrison says, looking surprised.

"Come on now, even if it does house an ultra-potent meteorite, I mean look at it. You'd have to crawl just to get inside," Mitchell says, still not impressed.

"Unless that's not the way in," Sandy says, thinking out loud.

Mitchell, connecting the dots faster than any of us, turns to Guida.

"Some of the caves, they're connected to it?"

Guida smiles as she nods.

"Connected to what?" Tom asks.

"To that monstrosity," Mitchell says, bringing our full attention to the tremendous rock-like structure now only about fifty yards away.

"An underground tunneling system?" Gregor asks Guida.

She glances at Harrison.

"She's unsure what you mean, but I would say yes, it's probably something like that," Harrison explains.

"How many of the independent caves scattered around the forest is that thing connected to?" Mitchell asks as we walk along.

"Just two. This one and one other."

"Well, it's something," Mitchell says, eying Tom. "To have a way in and out of that thing that puts us out in two different areas of this forest could be very useful."

Earlier, Gregor had found out that the huge structure

is not only resting along the water's edge but sitting on the planet's only land mass. One relatively small land mass surrounded by a vast body of water.

Walking up, everyone looks up in awe at the massive rock structure towering over everything else around it.

"It must be at least ten stories high."

Some of the bushes around us suddenly begin to rustle. Still feeling on edge from the run-in with that giant thing in the woods, everyone's relieved when the furry little animals from before scamper out.

"Looks like our friends have finished their escort," Mitchell says.

"You mean those little animals have been following us the whole time?" Gio asks, looking surprised.

"I would assume."

"Man, stealthy little critters," Tom says, seemingly impressed.

He's right, they are amazingly stealthy. I'd been listening on and off to the surrounding forest the whole time. Mainly listening for whatever that big thing is, but I never heard a thing. Nothing that would make me think there was anything, much less all those furry little creatures, anywhere near us.

All I can think now is: I'm glad they're nice.

"It's a baby one," Ava exclaims as she goes over and pets a tiny version of the little creatures.

"Holy shit, those suckers are cute," Tom says, smiling as the animals, still wary of the rest of us, allow Ava to touch and play with them.

"What is it?" Mitchell asks Harrison suddenly, moving next to him.

"I don't know," Harrison says, his hand on his head as he squeezes his eyes shut. Grimacing, he continues, "It's voices.

A lot of voices, but I can't understand anything they're saying. They're all jumbled—"

He glances at Guida as if surprised by something.

"Did she say something to you?" Tom asks.

"Not to me; to them. They're communicating with each other."

"Who? Who's communicating?" Tom asks.

"They are," Harrison says, looking toward the large structure as if surprised.

"I think they're all telepathic."

"Seriously," Mitchell says, seemingly irritated. For a person who likes to have control over situations, I'm sure being on a strange planet around aliens that communicate telepathically must rock his world.

"You can hear them?" Ava asks, surprised.

"I can, but I have no idea what they're saying. It's all just, like, sounds mixed with strange words."

"Is it similar to the Khoisan languages" Gregor asks, his interest piqued.

"Uh, Dad . . . I don't know what that is."

"Nobody knows what that is," Tom says sarcastically.

"It's an African language that consists of clicking consonants. They believe—"

"Yes, it can be quite similar to that language," Guida says suddenly, smiling at Gregor, as if tickled with him for making the connection.

"It can be?" Gregor asks, as if not following what she said.

"Can they also speak like you do?" Ava asks Guida.

"Yeah, out loud," Tom interjects.

"No. They have the physiology to do so, but speaking like this isn't something that's been done here in a very long time."

"How is it that you are able to talk, then?" Tom asks Guida.

Guida just smiles.

"She's different than the others," Harrison says, frustrated by whatever seems to be going on with his telepathic ability.

"I don't understand what they're saying. It's just a jumble of sounds in my head, but even so, I just feel like they think of her as someone special or something. They know she's here. Know we're here with her."

"Guida, you're changing," Ava exclaims suddenly.

"Holy crap!"

Again Guida's appearance has changed, but this time instead of a subtle difference like before, she's altered it so that she looks a lot like me.

"What the hell? How did you . . . ?" Tom asks, as if having a hard time wrapping his head around her looking so much like me.

"Altering your appearance in this manner is this something all beings on this planet are able to do?" Gregor asks.

"You'll find me unique, even among my own kind," Guida says.

"But why look like Jo?" Sandy asks, suddenly sounding concerned.

I know what he's getting at. Why change her appearance right now when we're about to meet the others of this planet?

"My outward appearance can be reflected by my inner thoughts," Guida says, then swiftly changes to look like Sandy.

No one can believe their eyes as a Sandy lookalike now stands before us. Not an exact replica, but close enough.

"What do you mean 'inner thoughts'?" Sandy asks, still not sure whether or not to be worried by the fact that she's taken on not only his image but, knowing Sandy, the fact that she's able to take on mine.

"She was showing the others telepathically what Jo looked like. Not telling them telepathically but showing them. It's very different, I think," Harrison says as if uncertain of his explanation.

"Showing them telepathically?"

"It's hard to explain, but . . ."

"You can explain it to us later, kid. Right now I'd like to know how we're supposed to get inside this monstrosity," Mitchell asks.

"I hope not that way," Reese says, looking way up at the top of the structure, at a stone ledge jetting way out from it.

"You must calm your mind to enter here," Guida says, motioning to some ivy.

Growing all around the structure in a thick layer is a strange-looking ivy covering the ground completely. Green leaves with distinct red and black lines running throughout make up a tangled mass of unbreakable-looking vines.

"It's like a quicksand type of thing. The calmer you are, the faster you sink, until you are through to the other side," Harrison says, trying to explain the process but still seeming to be battling the voices in his head.

"The other side. You mean in there?" Reese asks.

"Wait. You're telling us getting in there has something to do with that ground cover?" Tom asks pointing to the ivy.

"A single organism with sensory awareness," Gregor says as if amazed, which irritates Tom further.

"I don't care if it's an amoeba with an inferiority complex; I'm not going in there."

"Claustrophobic?" Mitchell asks, smiling.

"Claustrophobic . . . it's fucking plants!"

"What a wuss," Reese says, then abruptly steps onto the dense ivy.

Levi, without so much as a moment of hesitation,

follows. Why do I get the impression that's a common scenario for these two?

Guida doesn't seem surprised by the twins and their fearlessness. Honestly, I'm not, either. Since the moment they've joined our group, they've had a barrage of crazy situations thrown at them that they've tackled without even a moment of contemplation.

Honestly, for what we're here to do, that's an invaluable asset.

It only takes a second for Reese and Levi to sink enough that they seem unable to lift their feet back of the greenery.

"I'm friggin' stuck," Reese says, looking shocked at the circumstance she's found herself in all of a sudden. "Seriously, I can't move my feet."

"You need to focus. Calm your mind," Harrison says. "It can end up suffocating you if you move too slowly through it."

"What the hell?" Tom says, stepping away from the thick ivy.

Guida smiles at Tom, then steps onto it. Instantly she begins to sink and within a minute is gone, having passed through the vines as if it's the easiest thing in the world.

Levi, seemingly much calmer than his sister, begins to sink much quicker. Having sunk until the vines are up to his chest, he takes his sister's hand, then smiles at her.

"It's okay, just close your eyes and relax," he says to her, and as soon as she does, she begins to sink quickly until they're both gone . . . passed through the ivy to hopefully find themselves inside the huge structure.

"Why do I find myself stepping into weird-ass things with you people?" Tom says, right before stepping onto the ground covering himself.

Everyone else follows except Chi, Mark, Sandy, and me.

Since that monster thing could still be lurking somewhere out in the forest, I want to go last . . . and these three, as usual, refuse to leave my side.

I smile when I watch Harrison and Ava pass easily through the foliage. I would expect it to be a breeze for them. They're calmer than most of us even under stressful circumstances.

Tom, even though he was apprehensive before, is sinking through at a steady pace, even faster than Mitchell. Of course, he's not letting it go unnoticed, saying something about Mitchell not having a lot of mental strength.

"Whatever. I'll show you strength when I'm through this," Mitchell mumbles while trying to focus his mind on staying calm.

Chi, Mark, and I step onto the ivy. As soon as my foot touches the odd surface, I feel it grab me, instantly ensnaring me within its thick vines. Wanting to get this whole strange experience done with as quickly as possible, I close my eyes, concentrating on clearing my mind. As soon as I do, I hear it, that thing out in the forest. Its massive frame barreling through the trees, smashing tree limbs as it races toward us.

My eyes fly open. Sandy, standing on the edge of the ground cover, is watching me sink. As soon as he sees the look on my face, he knows something is wrong.

"What is it?"

"It's that thing, it's coming this way," I say, struggling to free my calves from the vines' ensnarement.

Chi and Mark, obviously much calmer than me, pass though the vines before they even realize the situation.

"Pull me out," I yell, knowing we need to get out of here, and there's no way I'd be able to calm myself now.

Sandy grabs me and tugs, but it's no use. I'm completely stuck in this web of overgrowth. As I hear its snarling, labored breath getting closer, I feel my body respond to the threat.

The energy within me blasts through the palm on my right hand, instantly charring the vines around my legs. Sandy yanks me out just as that thing crashes through the tree line, stopping at the edge of the clearing.

My breath catches in my throat. Sandy and I stand frozen in place as this massive beast stares us down. Easily larger than any land animal I'm aware of back home, this thing looks like a massively lethal variation of the little furry animals we saw earlier; the same color of fur and eyes, just a lot more teeth, claws, and attitude.

Growling, its black eyes are almost slits as it watches us. Even through its fur, I can see its rippling muscles contract as it sizes us up, ready to react to anything we might have the audacity to attempt.

"The cave," Sandy says under his breath, not moving a muscle. "Count to three, blast it and run."

It snarls at us then, and I can't help but wonder if it heard Sandy. Even worse, does it know what he said?

The cave is only about fifty yards away, and with our speed it shouldn't take us more than a few seconds to reach, but as I watch this beast eying us, I feel like it's going to be a few seconds too long.

I will the energy source within me to cooperate as I start to count. The palm of my hand stings as I reach the number two. A second later and I shoot out a blast of amber-colored energy toward the beast as we take off.

Running for my life, I don't look back—I can't. Reaching the cave, I dive for the entrance and pass through the narrow opening easily. Sandy follows right behind just as the beast hits the side of the rock, causing the whole cave to quake violently.

We've both made it inside without getting killed. We know it can't come in here; it could never fit though the opening.

Listening, I realize this isn't a typical predator, a huge box of rocks that only has its superior brawn to get by on. No, this thing is different. It's waiting right by the entrance, listening. I can hear its heartbeat like a heavy, distant drum, even . . . steady.

Standing up, I suddenly remember where we are. We're in the place Harrison called the mating cave.

6

—

feel the effects of this place right away.

There's a meteorite in here, like the portal caves, but it's different . . . stronger.

Strangely, even with the energy within me intensified by this powerful meteorite, I'm not feeling out of control in any way. No crazy surges, no weird fluctuations with my vision. Nothing. Could it be that the internal power instability that I've been dealing with lately is still tied to my emotions? To the same triggers I've dealt with ever since I changed?

Sandy doesn't acknowledge me in any way, just stands there glancing around. Although it seems like he's looking for something, I can't help but feel like he's just doing whatever he can think of to avoid me.

"We never really found out what they use this place for," I say, noticing some sort of strange structure off to the side, but really just wanting to say something, anything in the hope that we can get back to where we were before. Before he walked in on Mark and me, before everything got weird between us.

He looks right at me then.

"How well can you see in here?"

I just stand there staring at him, wondering why he's asking, but then it hits me. Other than right by the cave entrance, it must be completely dark in here to him.

Since I've been on this planet, I know my eyes have changed; heck, I've been dealing with it off and on the entire time. But with everything going on, I just never stopped to think about it, to think about what that could mean.

Now as I stand here, I realize when they changed I was left with more than just an acute sharpness in my vision. I was left with the ability to see in the dark.

"Like some cool, amber-tinted night vision," I mumble.

"What?"

"I can see everything," I say, suddenly noticing odd markings covering the cave walls.

"It's some type of huge pattern," I say, reaching out to touch it, before quickly pulling away.

"It's warm, really warm," I say, surprised, before tentatively placing my hand back on the wall to feel it again. "It's not just warm, it's . . . it's like it's electrified."

Sandy reaches out. As soon as his hand makes the connection, the entire wall seems to come alive.

Instantly we pull our hands away and step back, but whatever we did, whatever we started continues to happen all around us.

The same rich amber glow, like in the space portal meteorites, begins illuminating the entire cave, only this time the strange markings glow brighter, much brighter.

Noticing the unusual pattern seems to surround us, I begin to feel myself have a response, an emotional response.

"There's something about this place. I'm feeling . . . ," Sandy says, sounding strange as he trails off.

Glancing over, I notice he's turned away from me, but I don't need to see his face to know he's struggling with something. The set of his shoulders; the way his hands are balled into fists as they hang down by his sides. It's as if he's having some sort of reaction.

Pushing my own issues away, I'm suddenly concerned that something is really wrong with him.

"Are you all right?" I ask as I reach out and touch his arm.

Abruptly he steps away from me, from my touch, as if the subtle action is loathsome in some way. I feel the slight but am a little less hurt when I see that he's just as surprised with his reaction as I am.

"I'm sorry," he says, breathless, confused, as if trying to figure out what's happening.

"I know; it's affecting me too, making me feel . . . ," I stammer.

Under the light of the wall, he looks at me while I search for some way to explain what I'm feeling, what I realize now we're both feeling as we stand here staring at each other. As if we're both being affected by some deep-rooted feelings that are suddenly making their way to the surface.

I can't say anything, can't find the words. Not when having him so close is having such an effect.

I think it's concern I see in his eyes as he reaches out to me, but then I realize it's something else entirely.

The moment I feel his touch, he reacts, and I find myself pinned against the wall as his body, much stronger than I ever realized, pushes against me. I should get away, would be able to easily, but I can't. I can't move, can't think.

With his face inches from mine, my grasp on what's happening, on reality, begins to fade. All I can do is stay like this as I feel every cell in my body come alive as if for the first time.

Our eyes locked, he slowly lowers his head, seemingly just as entranced, as overcome as I am.

Pausing, he looks at me, and I know for sure. Whatever this is, whatever is happening to me, is happening to both of us. Maybe some sort of interstellar connection that's resonating from deep within us; I don't know, but whatever it is, I've never wanted anything more in my life than to have him kiss me.

Unable to withstand it another moment, the area between us begins to slowly close. I whimper slightly right before our lips touch. The moment they do, we freeze. Neither one of us is able to move, to breathe, as warm tingling sensations begin to course through our bodies. I pull away from the gentle softness of his lips, but the feeling within me only intensifies. We look at each other, surprised by what's happening.

He steps away from me so we're not touching anymore, not physically, but I can still feel him. Feel him as if he were all over me, deep inside me; warm, electric feelings moving within me, making not only my body come alive but my feelings for him as well.

As he moves toward me again, I react, flashing to another wall on the other side of the cave. I don't know why I moved away from him or even how I was able to, but something inside me snapped. Pushed my feelings for him away so I could think again, think like a person who has other realities in life besides whatever this thing happening between us is.

"Jo," he says to me, leaning forward against the wall, obviously still feeling the effects of our kiss.

I fight all the urges, all the ways my body is reacting to him, to this place.

"We need to get out of here," I say, looking away from him.

For a moment, neither of us says a thing, does anything. I will my body to try to snap out of it.

"You're right," he says, finally as if able to read my mind about this alien cave and its effects.

Trying to distract myself, I close my eyes and intently listen for that thing out in the forest.

"I don't hear the beast anymore, but I guess that doesn't mean he's not waiting for us somewhere out there," I say, still fighting that part of me that wants to stay here with him; to keep feeling the sensations our connection ignites within me.

"Guida said this place connects to the structure. We should go that way."

"That's right," I say, noticing another exit from this room leading into a dark cave tunnel. "It must connect through there."

"Then we should go," he says but doesn't move.

With his back to me, I can't help but wonder why he's hesitating so long.

"I can go first," I say right before noticing he isn't hesitating. No, there's something going on with him.

Blinking, he turns around, then starts to rub his eyes as if suffering from irritation.

"Is there something wrong with . . ." My breath catches when I notice a similar black pattern has formed on his eyes, on his human eyes. It's one thing to see my alien-like amber-colored eyes display a pattern, but to see it happen to completely normal-looking eyes, to Sandy's eyes, well, it just doesn't seem right.

"It's my eyes, I . . ."

"They're changing," I say, unable to wrap my head around what this could mean.

"What?"

"I think your eyes are . . ."

I'm unable to finish as I stand there shocked, watching as he begins to look all around the cave with full-blown alien eyes, eyes like Guida's, like mine.

"I can see everything in a way I've never been able to see before; it's incredible," he says, smiling at me. It's the first time in so long I've seen him smile; it takes my breath away.

"What's wrong?" he says, misinterpreting my reaction as he reaches for me.

"It's just that we need to get back to the others," I blurt out, dodging his touch. Ugh. It's been a while, but I see my ability to say or do the wrong thing at the wrong time hasn't evolved at all.

It takes him a minute to react. Normal Sandy would brush it off. Would be able to put it in perspective and move on, to say and do whatever it takes to keep me happy, comforted, to keep my mind in the game. But this isn't normal Sandy. This is new Sandy, filled with all sorts of feelings for me, like destiny just injected them into him.

"Sorry," I say, feeling terrible for ruining our first moment of normalcy since coming to this stupid planet.

"No, you're right; we should go," he says in a way that leaves me feeling like we're right back to where we were before coming into this cave, before experiencing whatever that was between us.

All I can do is nod as I follow him over to the tunnel.

"We're sure this is it?" I ask, feeling nervous as I stare down the dark, stony passageway.

"I don't see any other way out of here," he says, an edge to his voice.

"At least it's not creepy," I say, smiling, trying to keep the mood light.

Sandy doesn't smile back as he just stares at me for a moment, then without even a hint of emotion, he says, "We should go."

I nod, feeling hurt as I follow him into the tunnel.

As I walk along behind him, I'm surprised at how large the tunnel actually is. At how much work it would have taken to create something like this. Of course, that's with me thinking as a human from Earth. Who knows what Guida and the others on this planet are capable of doing. Maybe for them this would just be an afternoon chore. Like when my parents did their annual spring yard cleanup.

"Keep your ears peeled. We have no idea what could be in here with us," Sandy says, surly, making me wish we hadn't left the cave the way we did.

We're silent as we walk along through the tunnel. Plodding along as the weight of what happened between us earlier feels heavy in our thoughts. Even the occasional respite of thinking I'm hearing something up ahead doesn't dispel the heaviness of regret that lingers in the air around us.

"Still nothing?" Sandy asks quietly.

"Nothing," I whisper, trying to concentrate on the tunnel but feeling like this is all wrong.

"Wait."

"What is it?" he asks, alarmed, turning around to face me.

"I don't want it to be like this between us," I blurt out.

"Jo, this really isn't the time."

"I don't care. I know what that was back there. I mean after everything Guida's said, I know what it meant."

He stares at me for a moment, then turns and starts walking again.

Following behind him, I try to figure out what I want to say.

"It's just, with Mark and—"

"Jo, this is not the time," he says, that edge in his voice again as he continues to walk along.

"It's just, like you said, I need to keep my head in the game. I can't let my feelings for, for well, anyone, distract me from doing whatever it is I'm supposed to do here."

I hit a nerve. He stops walking and turns around. He goes to say something, then seems to think twice. Closing his eyes for a second, he sighs, as if trying to take control of his emotions. It's so strange to see him like this.

"You know I'd never want to distract you in any way from the prophecy, it's just . . . "

He stares at me as if searching for something.

"It's just, you must not feel it the way I do. I don't see how you could."

"Feel it?"

He sighs. "Jo, you're changing—you've changed. I mean it's obvious, but . . ." His eyes rove over my face. "But when it comes to me, to us and this thing between us, it just seems like you haven't changed, not the way I have."

Do I dare tell him how I really feel? How everything inside me is beginning to burn as I stand here staring at him while he confesses his feelings to me.

"I guess what I'm trying to say is that something inside me is different. I don't always have control over my feelings anymore when it comes to you. For the first time in my life, I honestly can't always think straight. So I'd rather not put myself in that situation; especially not now."

"What are you saying?"

Staring deep into my eyes, he says, "I'm just going to have to keep myself away from you as much as possible—physically, emotionally, away from you."

I want to argue. To tell him I need him by my side more than ever, but I can't. It just seems unfair to. Especially when our crazy destiny stuff is causing him so much grief. How can I not do whatever I can to alleviate it for him? After all he's done for me, I owe him that much.

"Well, if that's what you need to do," I say, frustrated. It's hard enough to stay focused on the big picture, on the prophecy and all the unknown situations that are looming in my immediate future, but to lose the one person I've had, and wanted right beside me since the beginning of all this, well, it's not just inconvenient. No, it's more than that for me—it's unbearable.

"It is," he says, lingering for a moment as he stares at me before turning and continuing on through the tunnel.

7

few minutes later, even as I'm still feeling the blow of his words, we begin to see a faint light coming from up ahead.

Sandy, pausing, turns to me.

"I know you want to get back to the others, but we need to be cautious. We have no idea what we're walking into."

I nod, knowing what he's getting at on all accounts.

Making our way to the light, we see that the tunnel curves sharply to the left. Pausing before we round the corner, Sandy stops and looks at me. Mouthing the word ready, he waits for me to nod, then walks ahead of me around the turn. A few steps and we find ourselves immediately entering another cave room.

My body surges slightly as I glance around at the odd display. All around the room are dozens of glowing rocks, like red-hot magma, casting a reddish glow throughout.

Similar to the cave Sandy and I were in, this one also has an unusual pattern etched into the walls. Not as large but just as interesting, unique. A bizarre pattern consisting of intertwined loops and sharp edges. As distinctive as it is seemingly inconceivable in its design, it's oddly familiar.

"I wonder what it is," I mutter to myself as I study the design, locking its image away in my head, feeling like it may be needed at some point later on.

"What do you think they use this place for?" I ask, noticing dozens of beautifully forged metal benches encircling what looks to be a hole in the floor, a deep abyss in the stone just big enough for a full-grown body to fit through.

"It's the same metal used to make that strange weapon Guida had earlier," Sandy says, running his hand gently over the smooth surface of one of the benches.

As I lean over and look down the deep hole, my body instantly reacts.

"There's a meteorite down there," I say, surprised. "It's not a strong one, but it's there."

"This room must be at the base of the giant structure," he says as he looks down the hole for himself.

"That's right. Guida had said her ancestors built the giant structure over a meteorite. I guess to serve some strategic purpose."

"We should go," Sandy says, pointing to another tunnel than the one we came in on the opposite side of the room.

Entering it, I'm surprised at how different it is from the one that brought us in here. As if it's actually used on a regular basis, this one is lined down its edges with sporadically placed lights. The same type of glowing rocks from the room. Although only a dozen or so run along the ground on either side, it's as if we're walking down a dimly lit runway.

Making our way through the tunnel, I think about the strange room.

Everything in there seemed structured, intentional in its placement. I don't know if it was seeing it cast in the reddish glow that made it all seem sort of creepy, but I can't help but imagine that place being used to perform sacrificial offerings. Like in the movies where a bunch of weirdos are all chanting something as they lower some tied-up, struggling girl into a huge flaming fire pit. Offering up a sacrifice just so they'll have a good crop or something the following year or, even worse, to keep some underground monster appeased. Whatever the reason, though, it's never justified.

"It's actually a spiritual place for them," Harrison says suddenly in my head, laughing at my observation.

"Harrison! Where are you?" I ask out loud, causing Sandy to stop abruptly and look at me.

"Guida says we aren't far from you. Just at the end of the tunnel you're in."

"They're not far," I say as we continue through the tunnel.

Just as I start to wonder if Guida's definition of "far" is way off, I see a sharp turn up ahead. Just like before, as soon as we make the turn we're walking into another room. A room full of aliens.

Shocked, I just stand there, unable to move as I look around the tremendous, cave-like great hall. With hundreds of beautiful bluish-green lights covering the walls all around us, these beings just stand there, silently staring us down.

Not sure whether I should be completely freaked out, I glance over at Sandy and see he's just as shocked as I am.

Somewhat humanlike, their faces are long and narrow, comprising the tiniest jaw and high, deep-set cheek bones. With a large forehead, larger than would seem appropriate, it's their eyes, piercingly black, that are the most distinctive. Without a doubt, it's their most pronounced feature.

They're tall and slender like Guida; there's a similarity I find striking, almost unsettling. Each and every one of them has an unusual design covering their bodies, even making its way up their necks and onto portions of their face; colorful art is etched onto the surface of their skin.

Seemingly more interested than threatening, they're an imposing sight as they stand there still, silent, watching us with such intensity that I find it hard to look at any one of them for long. Is it the prophecy thing? Is that why they're looking at us like that?

They have the same glossy black hair worn in one of two

distinct styles. I start to wonder if this is how they tell the females from the males. Other than that, there doesn't seem to be any other distinguishing feature that would suggest the sex of these beings at all.

A strange movement catches my eye. I notice it again and realize it's what they're wearing. At first glance it seems each of them is wearing clothes made from the same exotic material similar to Guida's. Looking closer, though, I realize it's different, a white fabric, seemingly thick and sturdy, but as soon as the wearer moves, it flows with them as if made of the thinnest, finest, shimmering silk.

A second later and there's a strange noise, barely a sound, but they all react. The entire sea of bodies in front of us all moves to either side of the giant room, like a parting of the Red Sea. It only took one second, one reaction, and now we find ourselves standing in front of an open area running directly up the middle to Guida, as if she orchestrated the whole spectacle.

Guida looks different yet again. This time she's a cross between the aliens standing all around me and the way she looked when she was on earth. It's like her special way of bridging the gap between our two worlds.

As we begin to walk toward her through the divide of aliens, I notice the floor is sloping up. The grooves in the gray rock material give me enough traction that the incline is more of an oddity than anything else. It's as if we are walking up, literally up, to Guida.

As we slowly make our way through the silent crowd, every eye seems to be on me specifically. I know what they're expecting me to do, I know why I'm here, but why do they seem so in awe? Their intense wonderment isn't just strange, it's unnerving.

The words chosen one pop in my head. How can they

not with the way they're looking at me? Should I revel in this celebrity status instead of just continuing to be perplexed with it all? Honestly, what kind of jerk would?

Drawn to their distinctive body art, I notice that every part of their skin that isn't clothed seems to have it—every part. Some of the patterns are similar, and even a few seem to be identical, but for the most part they are all very different in color and, most interestingly, design.

"Jo," I suddenly hear Harrison say in my head.

Looking toward Guida, I see him standing next to her and the others of my monumental team. A team that looks utterly relieved to see Sandy and me headed toward them.

Mark abruptly leaves the group. Without any regard to anything else around him, he heads my way, walking right through all the aliens until he gets to me.

"Are you okay?" he asks, his large frame coming right up to me as he reaches out and touches my arms. "What happened?"

Right away, I notice the aliens seem confused by the exchange.

"It was this huge . . . I don't know, beast thing that came out of the trees . . ."

"What?" Mark says as if in shock by my words.

"I'm fine, though, really. I'll tell you all about it later," I say, trying to backpedal as my thoughts instantly jump to Sandy and the cave. How will I be able to tell him that part? A monster after us in the forest, that's easy . . . but the other thing . . .

"Okay," Mark says, then sees Sandy and takes a double take. Without saying another word, he just takes my hand and we begin to walk through the crowd of aliens.

Once we reach Guida and the others at the top of the steep incline, everyone's shocked with the change to Sandy's appearance.

"Your eyes . . . what happened to you two?" Tom asks Sandy as Mitchell listens intently.

Uncharacteristically surly for Sandy, he gives a brief explanation of everything that happened to us, focusing mainly on the lethality of that thing that was trying to kill us, rather than what happened in the cave. Gregor thankfully speculates that the power source within the cave must have been potent enough to trigger Sandy's evolution.

"So you're one of the special ones with the eyes," Tom says, obviously mulling over what it could mean.

"Well, while you two were out there playing around," Mitchell says snidely, eyeing Mark, "vision boy saw that we are in fact going to have some time to prepare after all."

Harrison looks unsure. "It was just a quick vision of us training or something. Well at least Jo was, I mean; I mostly saw her. That's how I knew she would come back here, that she would be okay when she didn't come through the vines."

Guida, as if on cue, turns and without so much as a word looks out at the aliens as if she's going to say something, but she doesn't. No, she just stands there staring at them while they stare back at her as if amazed.

"They are amazed," Harrison says in my head. "They're amazed by us and what we're here to do."

"To save their world," I say.

"No, more than that . . . to fulfill the prophecy."

Before I have time to really think about what he said, five aliens step forward from the crowd and motion for us to follow them.

They lead us all out of the large room, and we find ourselves in yet another tunnel with the same bluish-green lights covering the walls. Glancing around the wide corridor, I can't help but think how different it looks than the tunnels Sandy and I were in.

Hanging along the walls is what looks to be instructional artwork, consisting of shiny gold fabric pieces displaying all types of complex-looking astronomical charts and schematics of the planet, drawn with what looks like muted-colored chalk.

Stopping our trek through the giant structure, we pause to get a look at some of the charts.

"I can't believe you're able to read these things," Tom says to Gregor as he stares at one of them.

"While you were gone ,Gregor and I came here. He was able to find out some information from these about the planet and such," Gio says to Sandy.

"Yes," Gregor says excitedly. "I was able to determine some of the planet's characteristics and other fascinating aspects of—"

"Yeah, but did you find out anything that could be useful to us?" Mitchell asks, knowing Gregor and his tendency to drone on and on about useless scientific facts.

"Well, this planet has no seasons, no changing from days to nights and vice versa."

"So it will never get dark," Mitchell says, as if contemplating what this will mean strategically.

"Not on this side of the planet."

"What do you mean this side?"

"This planet is tidally locked to its suns, so it doesn't revolve around them. It also doesn't spin or rotate, so wherever you are on the planet, the suns are in the same positions all the time."

"Hence no seasons . . . and no days and nights," Tom says as we all start to walk again through the tunnel. Walking along, we pass a multitude of exotic-looking plants lining the walls encased within long, narrow containers made of an odd-looking metal.

"Gregor was practically drooling when he saw those," I hear Gio whisper to Sandy, referring to the distinct beauty of a group of familiar purple flowers growing in one of the cases. "He was going on and on about them and the possibility of creating biological weapons."

Sandy, unexpectedly solemn, doesn't respond, which seems to bother Gio. Glancing around, I can tell she wants to say something but can't with all of us within earshot, especially me and my hearing.

"I would think the tidally-locked-to-its-suns thing is a win," Tom says more to Mitchell than anyone else. "If it's always day out, that's got to simplify things for us."

"Actually not at all," Gregor says matter-of-factly. "You see the simplicity of this planet's astronomical positioning may be astounding, but in essence, that's what makes it complicated," Gregor says, glancing back when he realizes the supply of informational charts and cases filled with foliage stopped a few feet ago.

"What are you talking about?"

"Solar weather . . . ," Gregor says, pausing for a moment. "Like what we were speculating about earlier."

"Solar storms with the possibility of dry lightning or superbolts," Levi says, strangely excited.

A few feet more and the entire floor begins to drastically slope up.

"Exactly; you see this planet has two suns of different sizes, and from what I could tell, they're rotating at different speeds."

"So?"

"Well, since the planet doesn't spin or rotate and is locked in relation to its suns, the same area, this area, would be affected most by any storms."

"Are you sure? I mean, what do suns have to do with storms?"

"Solar storms are created by the spin of a sun, which then determines the severity, duration, and frequency of each storm, so because this planet has two suns spinning at different rates, it—"

"Okay, we got it. So how do we detect them?" Mitchell asks.

"We can't. These are solar storms, so there's no way to determine when they'll happen or how severe they'll be when they do."

"So we're going to be dealing with unprecedented and unpredictable weather while we're here. That's just great," Tom says sarcastically.

As we make our way through this rocky structure, I'm surprised how steep the slope in the floor continues to be. Then it hits me: there are no stairs in here. I haven't seen stairs yet since we've come through the vines, which is surprising considering what I saw of this place from the outside.

"How far up are we going?"

"Hopefully all the way," Mitchell says, thinking strategically again.

Guida just smiles at him, seemingly enjoying him and his ways. Of course, she's the only one.

"So other than planets and weather, did those charts tell you anything about the type of tech we have to work with? Like surveillance systems or weapons?" Mitchell asks.

"Those charts didn't, but with storms of this magnitude there's no way they would be able to establish satellites or other systems anyway without them interfering with the readings or, most likely, destroying the equipment altogether."

"So they've been isolated to their own planet all this time?" Tom asks.

"I would think so," he says, then sees Guida smile at him as if she's enjoying all the discussion about her planet.

"If this was a problem we had on earth, we wouldn't have our Global Positioning System in place or any of the things we've established and come to rely on. Kind of makes you appreciate our sun and how well behaved it is," Gregor says, then chuckles.

"Great, so it's like the dark ages here," Tom says, as if in disbelief.

"Technologically speaking, yes, but what they lack in technology, they make up for in research. I mean, their, uh . . . ," he says, looking at Guida before continuing. "Your charts are just extraordinary. The most extensive and comprehensive charting of a planet, its suns—"

"That's great, but what we need is weapons, security of any kind, and maybe, I don't know . . . a plan," Mitchell says irritably.

"Well, remember, that's why you're here," Tom says without a hint of amusement in his voice.

Mitchell grunts, looking more aggravated than before. "What about enemy aircraft? Whoever we're going be fighting has to get here some way," Mitchell says with an edge to his voice.

"Of course, but during worst-case conditions, no aircraft of any kind would be able to fly around the time of these storms. Not these kind of storms."

"Yeah, well, we'll see about that," Mitchell says, seemingly not convinced.

As we continue to walk along, I begin feeling the calming effects the beautiful bluish-green hued lights are having on me as they light our way. Suddenly the passageway steepens drastically and curves sharply to the left. Feeling off balance, I find myself having to reach out and grab the wall to help me climb. To my horror, the minute my hand touches one of the lights imbedded in the rock, it moves. Yelling out, I react, moving as far away from the wall and whatever that was as I can.

"What is it?" Mark asks.

"The light; it's slimy, it . . . moved!"

"Oh," Mark says, then sighs as Ava and Gio chuckle.

"I forgot you didn't know about that," Mark says, smiling now.

"Oh yeah," Tom says grinning. "We found out earlier it's bugs all over the walls lighting everything."

"It's actually a type of light-emitting gastropod," Gregor says.

"Or what everyone else call slugs," Reese says.

"We have a species on earth that's similar," Levi says, surprising us again with his knowledge of random science facts.

"Aren't they amazing?" Ava says as she gets a closer look at one.

"Yeah, Josephine," Gio says sarcastically, smiling at me. "They're amazing, aren't they?"

"Amazingly gross," I say, looking at my hand to see if there's anything on it.

Although completely disgusting to my feminine sensibilities, it makes sense. I mean, did I honestly think that the aliens had somehow embedded lights in all the cracks within the rocks of this entire structure?

"No, these little guys are gorgeous," Ava says, checking on the slugs in the wall I inadvertently touched right before we start heading up again.

Finding the lights throughout the tunnel a lot less calming now, I make sure to walk directly in the middle of the narrow passageway as we continue to make our way through this giant structure. Mark and some of the others chuckle when they notice what I'm doing. At least it didn't freak me out enough to wake up the energy within me. I don't think anyone would be laughing if I started blasting the little suckers.

A few seconds later and the tunnel splits. Following the aliens into the one on the right, I can't help but notice that the other one seems more inviting. The walls in this one immediately narrow while the lights start to become more sporadic in their placement. As the tunnel becomes darker, the floor continues to slant up at a steep incline; unevenly placed stones become a constant tripping hazard, causing our pace to slow tremendously.

I find myself climbing right next to Ava, who starts inquiring about the beast Sandy and I had a run-in with earlier.

"I wonder why it would want to hurt you," Ava contemplates, seeming oddly perplexed that this massive, snarling predator would attack us.

Mumbling something about it probably just being the beast's nature, I notice the aliens listening intently to our exchange.

"Do they understand what I'm saying?" I ask Harrison in our special way.

"It's not the words you're saying that they're paying attention to," he says to me alone. "They're paying attention to everything else."

"Everything else?"

"Yeah, your tone, body movements . . . basically all the other ways you're communicating other than the words you're saying."

"Can they tell you and I are talking telepathically right now?"

"Uh, yeah, I'm pretty sure they can," he says, and then I notice all five of them are looking between Harrison and I as if completely intrigued by the two of us.

"Why do your markings match?" Ava asks two of the

aliens, motioning to the identical pattern covering their bodies.

Both of them, exhibiting the most pleasant demeanor, look down at where she's pointing to, then back up at her without making a sound. They seem to be enjoying the interaction without having any idea that she's actually asking them a question.

"Does it mean that they're related or that they're a couple?" Ava asks Harrison as if he's an expert.

"Uh, I'm not really sure," Harrison says.

"So how can you tell which one is the boy or the girl?" Ava asks, continuing with her interrogation as she smiles at the aliens.

Harrison glances at Guida as if in need of help.

She seems happy to oblige.

"You distinguish differences in each other based on physical characteristics," Guida says, causing all the aliens to quickly look at her. "Our distinguishing factors go much deeper than that."

Ava grins excitedly. "Much deeper . . . Well, I'm definitely going to want to learn more about that."

The walls, having been narrowing ever so slightly this whole time, have closed in on us so much we're all having to duck down as we go along.

Just as I start to wonder if crawling is in our future, we're there, at the top of this giant fortress of rock.

8

⸺

Around the size of a football field, it's astoundingly larger than any room I've ever seen. As I look around, my eyes are immediately drawn to the glassy black parallel lines running sporadically throughout the gray rock, each one reflecting a multitude of minute glimpses of every occupant within. It's like a million ultrathin mirrors covering the walls, ceiling, and floor, projecting to everyone inside the room the distracting effects of everyone's presence and their movements as well.

"Damn, this place is incredible," Reese says.

"I know, I've never seen anything like it," I say, realizing the reflective fissures and size aren't the only things that make this place so unbelievable. It's the fact that although most of it is securely contained within the walls of this enormous rock, the very end is out in the open. Literally outside.

"They're fulgurites," Levi says, glancing around the room in awe.

"Extraordinary. Obviously the result of the weather phenomena we discussed earlier," Gregor says.

"Fulgurites," Gio asks Levi specifically.

"Caused when lightning strikes a rock," he says as he traces his finger along one of the mirrored lines running through the stone. "It makes sense. I mean, rocks are naturally occurring electrical conductors, so—"

"So if one of those storms comes, you may not want to be hanging around in here," Reese says, seemingly irritated by Gio and her usual way of interacting with the members of the opposite sex.

"That's insane," I hear Ava say laughing, as Harrison and the other aliens stand at the entrance to the room. "That's not even a word; it's just a bunch of sounds."

"I know, right? Now you know why she decided to go with the name Guida," Harrison says, smiling.

"Harrison described it as big, but shit, this place is friggin' huge," Tom exclaims.

"Yeah, it's big but . . . ," Mitchell mutters as he glances around.

"What?" I hear Tom ask Mitchell under his breath.

"Nothing. Let's just get you misfits ready to fight," Mitchell says, glancing around the room as if devising the best strategy given the location.

"Misfits. Really? We're back to that again?"

"Considering I'm probably getting ready to die with you freaks, yeah," Mitchell says gruffly.

"Well, at least you got the pep talk down."

Ignoring Tom, Mitchell just stands with his arms folded, staring at each of us as if sizing us up.

"So, what can they all do? I want to at least know what I have to work with," he says to Tom.

"Some of their abilities are still progressing, but I have a pretty good idea. Of course, except for Jo."

"Don't worry, I know how to poke that bear if I need to," Mitchell says snidely under his breath.

"Uh . . . do you really want to poke a bear that could end up not even being a bear?"

"Always," Mitchell says, sneering at me.

Getting to the other side of the room, I find myself stepping out on a massive rock ledge extending well beyond the confinement of the cave.

As soon as I step out from under the ceiling onto the strange balcony jutting way out over the vast, foreign landscape far below, I glance around and get an overwhelming feeling that I've been here before. I recognize it. This giant ledge and the way the sunlight reflects off of the glassy fragments embedded within its rock.

My recollection of it seems like déjà vu or at the least some random dream. But I know it's not. No, it's the same ledge that was in the vision I shared with Sandy, then again with Harrison. The one where Ava was twirling around, the one with the two suns.

How is that possible? How was this place in two different visions I had back on Earth, back before we even came here?

"I'll be able to work with this terrain," Mitchell says, eyeing me snidely as he steps out to the very edge of the ledge. I guess it's his way of telling me to stop being a wimp and get my ass beside him so I can also get a better look at our surroundings.

"It's got to be part of our abilities," Tom says to Sandy as they come out on the ledge. "How else do you explain not being tired, or hungry for that matter? Shit, how long has it been since we've even eaten?"

Sandy and I lock eyes for a moment before he quickly looks away. Although I'm already used to his new look, I find it odd that no one has really talked more about his ocular metamorphosis.

"This is amazing. You can see everything from up here," Mark says, coming up beside me.

"Yeah, it's crazy. It seems that other than the ocean, lake, or whatever that is over there . . . ," I say, bringing his attention to the vast body of water off to the left of us, "it's all forest."

"Or so it looks that way," Mitchell mumbles to himself.

Ignoring him, Mark says, "Yeah, it just seems so similar to Earth."

"I know, it's crazy," I say, smiling, feeling reassured by the thought of it.

"But it's not Earth," Mitchell says, agitated as he looks between Mark and I. "Is it, Jo?"

"What's your problem?" Mark asks sternly.

"My problem is your afterthought," Mitchell says, suddenly turning toward Mark. "The sooner you realize you're not here on a vacation with your girlfriend, on some trip she invited you to come along with her on, the better."

"You think I don't know that?" Mark says angrily as he stands face-to-face with Mitchell right on the edge of the giant ledge.

I feel my pulse quicken, feel my body reacting to Mark being in that situation. Although part of me knows he's different now, knows he's changed, that he's not as vulnerable, I still can't help the way I'm reacting. I can't help the need to protect him at all costs.

Mitchell, noticing my reaction, eyes Mark for a moment, then backs down and starts to walk away.

"Just so you know, I'm rooting for the model-looking one," he says, then smiles at me. Not a friendly smile or even a smile that would tell me he wished it hadn't gone so far. No, this was a smile telling me that he planned this. That everything went exactly the way he wanted it to.

Headed back into the enormous room, he pauses when he gets by Tom.

"Bear's been poked. Now we can start."

A few minutes later and Tom's gotten everyone together on one side of the room. Mark, right beside me as Tom starts, is still stewing.

"So now that we're here, it's time to start preparing for this thing."

"How do we prepare for a prophecy we know nothing about?" Reese asks skeptically.

"Well, for some of you it's learning basic fighting skills," Mitchell says, ignoring her attitude.

"Basic fighting skills . . . are you kidding? Listen G. I. Joe, I'm not—"

"Reese," Levi says, then shakes his head at her.

"Look, it's got to help," Tom says, eyeing Mitchell. "But we're not just learning how to fight. No, you see we talked about it, and the way we see it, Jo chose each of us to be on this team for a reason. So what we really need to do is figure out why."

"I don't really know why," I say, thinking back to when I was branding everyone. How I really had no control over it.

"I know," Tom says as if reading my mind. "I'm pretty sure that's one of the reasons you chose me. I'm the one who's supposed to figure it out."

As Tom's words sink in, I realize he's right. If there's anyone here that can figure out why each one of us is here and what we're here to do, it's him.

"So I'm thinking Mitchell over there," Tom says nodding toward him. "He's got to be here because of his battle strategies, fighting skills—shit like that. I mean, it's pretty much all he does, right?"

"It's not all I do," Mitchell says, then looks right at Chi.

Chi doesn't move or look away from Tom, not even for a second. Not a look, not a flinch, nothing.

Mitchell, responding to her total lack of acknowledgement,

just smiles. A smile like I've never seen from him before, a real smile.

"So, before he gets killed," Tom says, glancing at Chi, "I think we should let him do his thing."

With a fluidity and skill that would take most people a lifetime to master, Chi and Sandy spar while everyone else stands on the sidelines watching. Even the five aliens, silent as they stand clustered together by the entrance to this room, seem apprehensive yet mesmerized by the display.

We're supposed to be learning. Getting ideas on how to fight in hand-to-hand combat if the occasion should arise. Of course all this is doing for me as I watch these two, especially Chi doing things that defy the laws of physics, is making me feel even more unsure about my whole part in all this. How can I help in this fight when all I have to offer is some energy source inside me that I really have no control over?

I feel it even now, as I watch them fight. Every move they make is reflected off of the hundreds of slivered mirrors contained within the walls of this monstrous room. Every sporadic flash of movement jolting my senses. Igniting this pent-up energy within me.

"Jo, I can tell this place is having an effect on you," Harrison suddenly says to me alone.

"It's the walls; they're so distracting when there's a lot of movement," I think, needlessly explaining what he already knows.

"I need you to focus on my voice. Not only on what I'm saying but on the tone of my voice."

"Okay."

"Like try and feel it, if that makes any sense."

I do and instantly feel calmer.

"Yeah, Guida said this is the room where you and I will gain control over your mind."

"Well, that doesn't sound weird," I think.

"No, not at all," he says, laughing in my head.

I can't help but chuckle out loud.

"Now that you're calmer, try to bring your energy to the palms of your hands, to just below the surface of your skin. I know it's hard with everything going on, but focus on my voice as you try to control the energy."

Watching the display before me, I do as he says and feel a slight tingle on my palms. Not the usual sting that tells me I'm probably about to blast someone. No, this is just a tingle, but enough to tell me that Harrison may be on to something.

"Yeah, let's hope so," he says right before Ava, not realizing he and I were connecting, starts talking to him.

Feeling much better now, I watch as Chi and Sandy spar like they've done it a million times before. It's strange; not only has Sandy adopted her fighting style, but surprisingly he is able to actually challenge her at times.

"See the things he's doing?" Tom says to Mitchell. "He wasn't able to fight anywhere near that way a week ago. All I can think is that it's an ability thing. Like he gained the ability to adapt or learn quickly or something."

"That would be useful," Mitchell says, not taking his eyes off them.

"I'd say so. Plus with his connection to Jo," Tom says absentmindedly, as if Mark and I weren't right by him, hearing his every word.

Mitchell knows and glances at Mark with his usual look of contempt.

"Hey, ninja girl," Mitchell yells suddenly, motioning for Chi to come over to him.

Chi quickly holds up her hand to stop Sandy from advancing toward her, then in a flash, she is standing right in front of Mitchell, brandishing one of her discs. Smirking, she extracts the blade.

While the speed and lethality of her actions are intimidating to the rest of us, they just seem to turn Mitchell's crank all the more.

"Imagining where you'd like to put that, aren't you?" Mitchell asks, obviously into her in his own revolting way.

"That's a good point," Gregor says all of a sudden, seemingly unaware of anything going on other than Chi's weapon. "What if her discs could emit a biological substance upon penetration of the target?" he says, going up to Chi and gently taking the disc right out of her hand before inspecting it.

I'm pretty sure if it had been anyone else trying to get their hands on one of her weapons, it would have been a different outcome, but it's Gregor, and not surprisingly, she seems interested in what he's saying.

"You mean a substance like what was in those flowers earlier?" Tom asks.

"Yes, the biological compound—"

"Could you also revamp a few of those things so that they detonate upon contact?" Mitchell interjects, instantly back to his no-nonsense gruff self.

"Possibly, depending on the materials I have to work with," he says, glancing at Guida questioningly.

"What about making it powerful enough to take out a multitude of targets at once?"

"Again, it's possible . . . but the stability of the device would most likely leave Chi vulnerable. That is . . . unless I can alter the activation of the mechanism itself," Gregor mumbles, continuing to examine the disc as he and Guida head out of the room.

Mitchell, his thoughts instantly back to the training, turns to everyone and says, "Okay, now let's see what some of the rest of you can do, preferably without killing each other."

"Preferably, really," Tom says shaking his head. "I don't think you're getting the whole team thing."

"Gio, you think you're a trained fighter. I want to see you up against one of the wild cards," Mitchell says, eyeing the twins, as if trying to figure out which one.

With her hands on her hips, looking more like a model waiting on her photo shoot to begin than a contestant in a sparring match, she smirks at him. "You really do have a talent for motivating."

"Well, that is a priority of mine," Mitchell says as he motions for Levi to come over.

Gio smirks as she watches Levi. Although not a complete Adonis like Sandy, he's handsome, with thick, dark hair and a muscular lithesome physique. Attributes never lost on Gio and her usual scrutiny when it comes to the opposite sex.

With his arms folded across his chest, Tom says to Mitchell, "I guarantee this will show us more than their fighting skills."

Like a big cat giving off a vibe of disinterest right before pouncing on an unassuming prey, she saunters over.

"So, Levi," she says, smoothing her impossibly gorgeous hair down around her head, "have you ever been physical with someone who wasn't your sister?" She flashes him a seductive smile.

Levi doesn't react in any way as he just stands there, watching the display.

Turning to Sandy, she smirks. "I guess that's a no."

"Just hit the bitch already," Reese yells at her brother.

He does and quickly lands a perfect jab to her face.

Anger, or something altogether different, flashes across Gio's face as she licks the blood from her lip.

"Now you're just turning me on," she says, then quickly goes to throw a punch.

Raising his arm, he attempts to block the strike just as her true intention makes its connection. As the brute force of her kick hits the side of his face, his entire body is thrown to the side.

Before she has time to continue showing him the ramifications of hitting her in the first place, she finds herself being tackled from the side with such a force that she and her assailant land in a heap on the ground.

Reese, a slew of profanities streaming from her, punches Gio repeatedly while attempting to get her in some sort of hold. If rage was a useful fighting technique for anyone other than the Hulk, then Reese might be able to dominate her, but Gio easily breaks free, punching Reese in the face hard enough to stun her, before leaping to her feet.

Raising her foot, she attempts to deliver a kick to Reese's head, but just before she does, Reese is gone, instantly vanished into thin air only to be replaced a second later by her brother.

Levi, not stunned like his sister, easily catches Gio's leg in his hand, then swiftly pushes it up, sending her flying backward before she lands on the ground with a thud.

Undeterred, Gio immediately leg-sweeps him, causing him to fall to the ground, where he lands right beside her.

"Okay, that's good," Mitchell yells out.

"I always knew I'd get you on your back one way or another," Gio says to Levi as she gets to her feet.

Mark suddenly touches my arm.

"Jo, I think something's wrong with Harrison," he says,

drawing my attention to Harrison, who's standing far off on the other side of the room.

Hearing my concern about his mental state, he looks right at me.

"I'm good," he says, then touches his head as if in pain. "It's just kind of crazy in my head right now."

"Crazy?"

"It's the aliens. The fighting is either freaking them out or making them really excited. I don't know."

I relay the message to Mark as I glance at the aliens. Freaked out? Excited? Other than the fact that they've made their way more inside the room, they don't seem to be acting any different than they have been the whole time.

"Maybe not, but their thoughts are."

"I gotta say, that was fun to watch," Mitchell says condescendingly, bringing my attention back to the sparring, "but how about I show the three of you some ways to do more permanent damage when you get your buttons pushed?"

9

—

A few minutes of watching them train under Mitchell's tutelage, and I quickly realize that his methods, although crude and usually painful for anyone involved, are having the desired effect. They're picking up fighting techniques that are so simplistically lethal that I can't imagine how knowing them wouldn't be beneficial for anyone.

Along with the specific techniques, they're also being challenged in such a way that if they did have abilities lying dormant within them, unrealized and even more thrilling for Mitchell, untested, it's probably only a matter of time before they're pushed to such a degree that they'll unconsciously delve deep inside their bag of tricks to claim them.

Harrison, seemingly getting a reprieve from the aliens' telepathy for the moment, is far off on the other side of the room, away from all the fighting, watching intently as Ava, in her quest to get the aliens to say something, is delighted when one of them finally makes a sound. Not a sound that would be even remotely close to a word, but for how excited Ava is they might as well have recited the Gettysburg Address. The entire interaction is so sweet, all I can think is for such an intimidating looking species, the aliens really are quite pleasant.

"No, it isn't anything like that," I hear Levi say then. "We're just really good at knowing what each other thinks and feels."

"I'm not so sure about that," Mitchell says. "Something

about you two is off. I see it in the way you fight."

"You're twins, so your abilities have to be connected somehow," Tom says, eyeing them as if just looking at them could give him all the answers.

Levi glances at Reese, then says, "We can feel each other's physical pain, emotions . . . things like that."

"Levi, what the hell," Reese says irritably.

"I know, but it's something that could help."

"We can help without telling these fucking strangers everything about us," Reese says, glaring at him.

"So are you feeling that she's pissed right now?" Mitchell asks Levi snidely.

Reese, suddenly in a rage, looks as if she's about to hit him.

"Just go ahead and keep pissing people off. I guarantee you that if Jo doesn't end up taking you out, then being on this planet, with the kind of lightning that can cause all this"—she motions toward the hundreds of fulgurites dispersed around the area—"my brother will."

Levi looks shocked, knowing the clue within her threat wasn't missed by anyone.

"So that's your link with all this . . . ," Tom says excitedly. "Something to do with lightning?"

Levi shrugs while Reese looks sorry she ever said anything.

"Why wouldn't you tell us about your connection with the storms?" Sandy asks him.

"Even if I have been struck by lightning too many times to count, I don't see how that could help us."

"Really, you don't? We just happen to be on a planet that can have a crazy amount of lightning, and not only is it attracted to you, it doesn't kill you. You don't really see how that might be useful?"

"Normal lightning sure, but superbolts . . . Let's just say

if I get struck by one of those, I'm just as dead as the rest of you."

"You think so, but I've found when it comes to all this prophecy stuff things aren't always so black and white."

"Well, it's not necessarily something I think I should test out," Levi says, not sounding convinced.

"You know what I think? I think we need to have a little brainstorming session with Gregor."

"Great, you guys do that. I'll keep working here," Mitchell says, glancing at Mark and me.

Tom laughs. "I didn't mean now. There's no way I'd leave you to do anything with Jo or Mark. I mean, we can't fight as a team if we don't have a team."

Mitchell smirks, then turns to Gio. "Okay then, I'll have you work with the boyfriend to see if there's anything he can do other than get under my skin."

Tom shakes his head as Mark glares at Mitchell.

As Gio and Mark go over to another side of the room, Mitchell turns to me.

"You know, I get the feeling she's more than happy to work with him on just about anything."

"You really do have a death wish," Tom says to Mitchell, giving him a knowing look.

I shrug off Mitchell and his insinuation, thinking about what Tom said. With the energy within me so unstable right now, he's right. Having someone try and teach me fighting techniques could be deadly—for everyone.

I turn to Sandy, knowing that no matter what's going on between us he usually has my best interests at heart.

"I know I don't have any real fighting skills, but I'm not sure if I should be sparring anyone right now."

Ignoring me completely, he turns to Tom. "I've noticed Harrison using the connection he has with Jo to help her try and gain a better control over her abilities."

"How do you know he's been helping me?" I ask surprised.

Has he been watching me? Watching me so closely that he was able to pick up on the subtleties of conversations I'm not even having verbally?

Brushing me off again, Sandy goes on to say, "I think it's something they should continue working on while she trains."

"No way," Mitchell says. "Even if he did manage to find her off switch, do we really want to rely on some boy to keep her in line when the time comes?"

"Yeah, but now I can't help but think that may be one of the reasons that boy is here," Tom says.

"Of course, why wouldn't the codes to our nuke be in the hands of some pubescent teen," Mitchell says sarcastically.

"Exactly," Tom says, grinning.

"You know, your nuke's standing right here and can hear everything you're saying," I say, pissed about the way they're talking about me like I'm not even there and by the way Sandy's acting.

Feeling hurt and vulnerable, I find my thoughts wandering to the first time I ever saw Sandy; this new guy in school, visibly perfect in every way, making his way down the hall through a sea of gobsmacked adolescents. As he passed, he had smiled at me. Nothing earth-shattering, at least not to me. It was just a smile, a small recognition between two random people. How could I have known that someone I had such a minor exchange with back then was destined to play such a significant role in my life?

"Sorry, Jo, our bad," Tom says, glancing at me oddly as he interrupts my thoughts.

I hear Gio laugh then, and glancing over, I see her and

Mark sparring. Surprisingly enough, Mark seems to have already progressed enough in his abilities that he's able to hold his own. Even without any special moves, he's so large that his size alone carries is leverage.

As I watch them, it's like they're both enjoying the process, but for entirely different reasons. Mark, just as gung ho as ever when he's able to use his abilities, seems to be excited by the things his body is capable of doing, while Gio just seems excited by him period.

"Okay, well let's just get on with it, then," I say, suddenly impatient, wanting to do anything but stand here.

I feel Sandy's gaze at my change of attitude.

"Yes, Sandy, get on with it," Mitchell says with an edge to his voice.

"Why don't you teach me something yourself?" I say to Mitchell, all of a sudden feeling more than up to a challenge.

Mitchell laughs. "I don't think so, and since I know what's happening here, I'm going to go to the other side of the room since I'd rather not get hit by one of your stray death blasts."

"Trust me, if you're hit by one, just know it wasn't a stray," I say, sick and tired of his venomous remarks.

"I told you she was going to end up taking him out," Reese says to Levi, then leans in to say something else, but he pulls away. I guess he's still mad at her for earlier.

"You sure you're up for this?" Sandy asks.

"Of course, why wouldn't I be?" I say as I hear Mitchell make a snide comment to Gio from across the room.

"Because you seem agitated."

"I'm agitated because you're not getting on with it."

"You're agitated because your head's not in the game," he says sarcastically, stinging me with his attitude.

"What?"

"It's like I said before, you can't be so easily distracted."

"I'm not."

"Oh, really, you sure about that?" he says folding his arms across his chest.

"Okay, well, maybe I am distracted by you being such an ass."

"An ass? Really?" he says condescendingly. "I'm pretty sure it has nothing to do with me and everything to do with what's going on over there."

"It's like foreplay with those two," I suddenly hear Mitchell say right before noticing that he, Gio, and Mark are watching Sandy and me argue.

Appalled that he said that in front of Mark, I glare at him.

Just then I sense a shift in the air around my face right before I feel a smack to the side of my head, followed by another smack to the other side of my face. More dazed from the speed at which he landed the hits than the hits themselves, I shake them off.

"See what I mean? Easily distracted," Sandy says patronizingly.

"Did you actually just attack me?"

"Attack you? Are you serious?" he says, staring at me in feigned disbelief.

"You hit me. In my book, that's attacking someone."

"That's absolutely ridiculous. I'm trying to prove a point."

"What, that you getting your feelings hurt equates to me needing to watch my back when I'm around you?"

"Watch your back . . . are you kidding me? Jo, I'm here to help you get prepared to fight, not to hang out and mull over the insecurities you have about your boyfriend."

"Are you kidding?" I say, pissed. "You're going to talk to me about insecurities . . . you?"

Irritated, he pauses, then sighs. "Jo, listen. Regardless of what I may think or feel, at the end of the day, I know I have a job to do. That I'm here for a reason, a very important reason."

"Yeah, I know, to save the world," I say.

"No, you're here to save the world Jo. I'm here to save you."

Before I have a chance to grasp what he just said, I suddenly hear a loud thud and grunt from across the room.

Mitchell, doubled over, is down on one knee struggling to catch his breath.

"Just keep running your mouth," Mark says, his fists clenched as he stands over him.

"Oh shit," I hear Tom say under his breath.

Hunched over, still trying to recover from the blow, Mitchell shakes his head and chuckles slightly.

Mark, clearly pissed, continues to stand over him, his massive frame tensed, as if expecting retaliation at any moment.

Even as Mitchell begins to laugh, an odd, raspy, deep-throated laugh that sends chills down my spine, Mark doesn't back down, doesn't stop looking like he wants nothing more than for Mitchell to stand up and challenge him.

"I don't know why you're laughing. With things a little more even now—"

"Boy . . . ," Mitchell says, still doubled over but breathing more normally now. "That was a sucker punch. I'm about to show you how even we're not," he says, then, with a brutality only Mitchell could muster under the circumstances, he smashes his fist into Mark's kneecap, sending him crashing to the ground.

I feel the energy surge within me as rage courses through my body.

Harrison's beside me suddenly, reaching out to me. The second I feel him touch my forehead, all my emotions dissipate, instantly wiping away my rage as if dissolving it completely.

A moment later and Harrison falls to his knees beside me, his nose bleeding as he grabs the sides of his head.

Physically, emotionally, I feel numb, unable to help him or Mark in any way. Somewhere deep down I know I need to, or at least want to, but find myself unwilling to organize my thoughts enough to try.

Not able to wrap my mind around what's happening, I suddenly hear an agonizing groan. Mitchell, lying in a fetal position on the floor, has his head in his hands, as if in incredible pain.

"Harrison," I hear Tom yell just as my emotions begin to ease back into my reality.

Mark runs to his brother just as Guida and Gregor hurry back into the room. It's probably the connection Guida has with Harrison. Like a telepathic heads-up when something bad is going down.

Mitchell, as if his agonizing pain has already faded, just sits on the ground looking shell-shocked from the whole experience.

"What did you do to him," Mark asks his brother, as if trying to wrap his mind around Harrison's ability.

"I don't really know. I had to stop Jo, and then I saw him about to hit you again so I . . . I don't know, it just happened so fast."

"Are you all right?" Ava asks, quickly coming up beside him, looking upset.

"I'm fine," he says, swiftly wiping the blood from his nose on the tail of his shirt, then giving her a sweet smile.

"What happened?" Gregor asks Harrison hurriedly.

"What happened is I just found out your son has a few tricks up his sleeve," Mitchell says, completely healed and looking as though he's oddly happy.

"You were able to induce pain in someone with just a thought," Gregor says, looking at Harrison as if not surprised at all.

"You knew he could do that?"

"I thought it might be possible given the abilities he's already exhibited."

"So what else can you do?"

"I didn't know I could even do that," Harrison says not liking all the attention directed at him all of a sudden.

"What are they doing," I ask when I see Guida and the other aliens out on the stone ledge staring up at the sky.

"Oh right, that's why I was coming here in the first place. To tell you they're coming," Gregor says, then looks around at everyone just standing there staring at him as if he were expecting more of a response.

"Um, the prophecy, the beings we're supposed to save the world from . . . they're coming," he says, then seems satisfied when we all start running for the ledge.

The second I find myself outside with the others and feel a sudden emotional onslaught, I know for sure that Harrison's touch has completely worn off.

"Shit, it's starting," Tom says as we all just stand there, mouths agape, staring up at the sky.

Earlier there wasn't anything there, but now there's a barrage of black objects dotting the horizon.

I glance around at the others. At my team. The people I've chosen to fight with in a battle I still can't seem to wrap my head around. The same people I chose to stand with me, right now, on this massive stone ledge and watch as these things, these invaders, begin to make their way closer to us.

Ava grabs Harrison's hand just as Chi reaches into her jacket to grab onto one of her own objects of security. The twins glance quickly at each other, then back to the bombardment just as Mitchell, clenching his fists tightly, swears under his breath.

It's as if everyone, seemingly mentally preparing themselves for what's about to happen, can only stare upward, not able to take their eyes off the things rapidly progressing toward us.

Sandy's suddenly beside me, and even though I feel my body surge, it's his presence that reminds me of my role in all of this. Of the expectation that I'm not just a part of a team, that the power I'm starting to feel course through me is there for a reason.

We all watch as within seconds the objects are almost to us. Too small to carry anyone, they just look like small black pods falling from the sky and falling fast.

"What the hell?" I hear Mitchell mutter under his breath as a few of them land on the ledge, while others whiz past on their way to the ground below. I watch as they land sporadically all around the forest, littering its green backdrop with an array of small black dots.

Gregor reaches out to grab one, the scientist in him more interested than wary.

"Dad, don't," Mark yells right before beams of green light start streaming out of each of the podlike objects.

Chi quickly jumps to the side, able to avoid being touched by the beams, while the rest of us find our legs caught in the rays. Harmless, the light from each pod seems to pass right through us before connecting to the other pods to form some sort of light grid between them.

"Uh, should we be concerned?" Tom asks loudly.

Gregor puts his hand in and out of one of the light beams.

"Could be a scanning mechanism," he says, watching as it shifts its light around his hand, reacting to his movement.

"They're doing a preliminary sweep of the area. Smart. That's exactly what I'd do if I were about to invade a foreign land," Mitchell says glancing up at the sky.

"Yeah, but how is the information being communicated?" Gregor says under his breath, looking at it as if he wants nothing more than to grab one of the things up and start taking it apart to figure it out.

"Maybe a transmitter of some type," he mutters on, his interest even more piqued.

"I wouldn't touch that thing if I were you," Tom warns.

"No, of course not . . . ," Gregor says as if it's the last thing he'd do.

". . . at least not while it's in an active state."

I glance down off the ledge to the ground below. Like a blanket of lines, the same rays of green light stream from each of the pods, connecting them all in a complete area-wide grid system. For as far as I can see, stretched out across the area is a pattern of horizontal and vertical light beams.

"If they're sweeping, that means they're definitely planning on coming," Mitchell says.

Something suddenly catches my eye on the ground below. Was it movement? I stare at the ground, searching.

"What is it?" Sandy asks, noticing my sudden interest in the ground below us.

"I don't know . . . ," I say, my eyes distracting me. I blink away their annoying disruption of my eyesight and am left with that familiar sharpness in my vision. One that I normally could care less about but now am glad I have.

"I thought I saw something."

"Um . . . any of you notice the wind?" Tom says nervously.

Although I've been distracted, he's right—the air around us had really begun to come alive over the last minute.

"A storm," Mitchell asks Guida pointedly, probably wondering the same thing I am. Is this an actual storm or something else entirely?

Ignoring him, Guida looks down at the pods on the balcony. She's contemplating something, but what?

Gusting, the wind suddenly causes my hair to twist around violently.

"Is it me, or is the wind getting stronger?" Tom says, eyeing Gregor.

"What is it?" I hear Reese say suddenly.

Levi, holding his hands out in front of him, is studying them as if something's happening.

"Static electricity," he says, then instantly looks up to the sky.

"Lightning?" Reese asks.

"You need to get away from me," he says all of a sudden, stepping to the side of the ledge to distance himself from her.

"So it is a storm," Mitchell says.

"Fulgurites," Levi says under his breath as he glances around, seemingly lost in indecision.

"What?" Reese asks him.

"I can't be here," Levi yells to Reese as the wind gusts around us suddenly.

"Where the hell do you think you're going?" Reese yells back.

Levi, eyeing the edge of the balcony, suddenly lifts his hand as if shocked by something.

"Levi, no," Reese yells, but before anyone can do anything, he sprints to the end of the stone ledge and leaps off. The second his feet leave the stone ledge, he's hit by a bolt of lightning with such a force that it sends electrical currents ricocheting from him in all directions.

My senses stunned, I suddenly find myself flying through the air, shocked, unable to believe what's happened just as a tremendous crack reverberates all around.

Seconds later, I slam to the ground.

10

—

As a monotonous hum fills my head, I just lay there with my eyes closed, unmoving, agonizing pain coursing through my body.

Forcing my eyes open, I look up at the sky and realize this isn't the kind of lightning storm we're used to. Although the wind is gusting, there isn't any other indication that we're even in the middle of a storm. No clouds of any kind . . . just a typical sunny day.

There's another crack, and as if on cue, my ability takes over. Quickly, more quickly than I would have thought possible, my body begins to heal. I start to feel the pain subside as my heart rate steadies.

All of a sudden I hear someone running up.

"Jo," Sandy says, suddenly beside me, looking down at me worriedly.

"I'm fine," I say, sitting up.

Breathing a sigh of relief, he just stares at me for a few seconds before quickly snapping out of it.

As he helps me to my feet, I notice I've been blown completely off the ledge of the huge boulder and have landed far away in the thick vegetation of the alien forest. The pods, still connected by rays of light, lie sporadically all around the area.

"What about Mark?" I ask frantically, suddenly remembering he was right beside me on the ledge.

"I don't know. I jumped, then came right to you."

Desperately, I scan the area around us.

"Over there," he says just as a bolt hits a tree off in the distance. As pieces of bark go flying in all directions, we hear the crack and take off.

My heart drops the moment they come into view. Mark's on his back swathed in beams of green light, while Gio looks down at him, her long, silky, dark hair being blown around by the wind.

As soon as we get to them, Gio looks at us, her tearstained face a mask of anguished despair. I know I should be taken aback by this testament to her love for him, but I can't. Not now, not with him lying there, unmoving.

Falling to our knees beside him, Sandy checks to see if he's breathing while I try to stay calm and keep that thing resting deep within me at bay.

"He was struck," Gio says with an edge to her voice, causing Sandy to look at her oddly.

"His breathing is shallow, but he is breathing," Sandy says, eyeing me.

I place my hand on his chest, feeling it rise and fall ever so slowly just as Gio turns her back to me, as if trying to collect herself.

Levi runs up to us then, and although he seems out of breath, he looks completely healthy otherwise. How can that be?

"Is he all right?" he asks about Mark, serious-minded.

"He will be," Sandy says, giving Levi an obvious once-over.

"Yeah, I know," Levi says, looking aggravated. "Guess I'm lightning guy."

"So it doesn't affect you at all?"

"No, but this lightning isn't much stronger than what I've dealt with before. Plus, if I run fast enough, it misses me every time."

"So I take it these aren't superbolts," Sandy says.

Levi chuckles slightly. "Not even close."

"What about your sister?" Gio asks, looking oddly vexed. "She seems like the type of girl that would be unreasonably worried about her brother right about now."

"Reese knows I'm okay," he says matter-of-factly, then glances at his hands. "I better go," he says, then takes off.

A minute later and a massive bolt strikes the ground far off to the right of us. As sparks and pods fly through the air, a huge section of the green laser light grid explodes under the onslaught of the electric current. The entire grid short-circuits, and I watch as all at once all the green light beams go out.

Mark, opening his eyes, takes a deep breath just as another nerve-racking crack reverberates through the sur-rounding area.

"You're okay," I say, smiling down at him.

"Of course," he says in a low voice, giving me a weak smile back.

"Can you move?" I ask, suddenly distracted by some-thing out in the woods.

Standing up, I listen as the wind blows through the trees all around me. Concentrating, I hear the familiar terrifying sound of a slow steady heartbeat. The heartbeat of the last thing we need to deal with right now. Although close by, it doesn't seem to be moving. Like it's just sitting there, waiting.

"I hear the beast from before," I say, alerting the others to how much worse our predicament has just gotten.

"Where?"

"Over that way," I say, nodding in the direction of the beast's steady rhythmic heartbeat. "It doesn't seem to be moving, though."

"The structure's that way," Gio says, eyeing Sandy.

"Guess I should stop lying around," Mark says then, grunting as he sits up.

"Mark, wait, you need—"

"I'm fine. I've healed enough," he says, trying to reassure me.

Gio glances worriedly at Mark, then asks me, "Can't you kill that thing?"

"I don't know. Maybe if I was mad enough," I say, thinking about how connected the energy has always been to my emotions.

Sandy looks at Gio as if aggravated by her inquiry.

"We can't just rely on Jo's energy. We have no idea what the meteorites have done to the wildlife here. For all we know, that thing could have abilities, too."

As Sandy and I help Mark to his feet, I feel on edge as the wind causes continual movement all around us. Scanning the surrounding forest, I spot Levi headed our way.

"We should get inside somewhere," Sandy says.

"We won't be able to go in the same cave as before," I say, knowing it's not a logistical option but just stating the obvious, as having both Mark and Sandy in there at the same time would definitely cause some problems.

"No, we'll have to head away from the structure for now, then figure out what to do next," he says.

Levi walks up, completely unaware of our new plight.

"Glad to see you back on your feet," he says to Mark, as if feeling guilty that he was struck in the first place.

All at once, a crackling noise starts coming from the pods scattered all around us.

"What are they doing?"

"It sounds like they're short-circuiting," Levi says right before the crackling turns to popping. A few seconds later and there's a slight hissing noise as the pods start to disintegrate.

"What the hell?" Mark says as we all watch the pods start to liquefy until they're nothing more than a pile of goo.

"I take it they're done scanning," Levi says.

"I guess so," Mark says.

"Makes you wonder what's going to happen next," Levi says, glancing up at the sky for a moment before turning his attention back to us.

"Listen, you guys better get back. Go ahead through the vines. I'm going to wait until the storm's over."

"About that," I hear Sandy say just as something triggers the energy within me.

Concentrating, it only takes me a second to know.

"It's headed this way!"

"What's headed this way?" Levi asks.

Ignoring his question, Sandy quickly asks him, "Did you see any small caves toward the water?"

"Uh, yes . . . one," Levi says just as we start to hear something huge crashing through the forest toward us.

"We're going to need you to show us," Sandy says urgently.

Levi nods, then takes off.

Swiftly, we maneuver through the forest, following Levi with the beast crashing through the trees right behind us.

Just as I begin to hear its labored breath closing in on us, a cave comes into view. Only slightly bigger than the last one Sandy and I sought refuge in earlier, there's thankfully no way that monstrosity will be able to follow us in there.

"Keep going," Levi yells suddenly as he stops and stares at the forest behind us.

A few seconds later and I flinch as the bolt hits somewhere right behind us. Looking back, I see that Levi, now bringing up the rear, doesn't seem fazed at all. I guess you dodge enough lightning bolts and even that can become routine.

Just as the crack reverberates all around, we find ourselves coming up on the entrance to the cave. With a thick web of overgrowth covering most of the entrance and surrounding rock, I can only assume the aliens haven't used this cave in a while, if ever.

With the last lightning bolt having deterred the beast, we're able to hurriedly start pushing past an outer layer of thorny plants. As we make our way further through the dense vegetation, my arms and hands begin to sting from what feels like a hundred tiny cuts.

"So obviously nothing's come in here for a while," Gio says, looking irritated and completely out of place as I watch her, in her designer clothes and overall posh persona,

fight her way through the foliage.

Once we're all safely inside, we stand quietly, listening to the beast's labored breathing as he runs up to the cave. Unlike before it doesn't hit the side of the wall or act aggressive in any way. It just stays there for a moment before he just seems to give up and leave.

"I think he's leaving," I say, hearing the beast's heartbeat getting fainter.

"Well, that's very undramatic," Gio says.

Unlike the dark cave Sandy and I were in earlier, this one is surprising, lit on the inside from sunlight streaming in through various holes in the stone ceiling.

"I should probably move away from these openings," Levi says, looking up at the sky through one particularly large hole.

"Whoa, be careful, it's slippery in some spots," Levi says, referring to some sort of moss-like plant covering large portions of the stone throughout.

"So, what's the plan for us getting back without running into that thing again?" Gio asks.

"If we wait until the wind's died down, maybe I'll be able

to hear it better," I say, hoping to get a better handle on my abilities. It just seems any distraction, and I'm useless.

Mark, as if detecting my aggravation with my inability to meet my own expectations in all this, smiles at me reassuringly.

"Um, I think you guys may want to come see this," Levi says, his voice coming from another area in the cave.

Making our way to him, we walk around a small dark corner that leads to an enormous wide-open area.

"What's that smell?" I ask, noticing a particularly foul odor.

Covering my mouth to block the stench, I glance around, half-expecting to find dead things lying about. With a few small holes in the ceiling letting in just enough sunlight that it casts an eerie perspective on the scene, I soon realize that my assumption is reality.

Piled over to the side of the giant cave room is what looks to be a plethora of bones and rotting carcasses.

"So now we know why it reeks in here," Gio says.

"This must be its den," Sandy says glancing around.

"Great. We found its lair. No wonder it didn't need to chase us in through the thorny entrance," Gio says, looking around in horror.

"It must be able to get in here from somewhere over there," Mark says, nodding to a dark opening off to the side of the room.

"Jo, keep your ears peeled," Sandy says all of a sudden. "This could have been its plan all along."

Gio quickly gives Sandy a look.

"What is that thing?" Mark asks Levi, noticing him checking out a tremendously large skeleton of some fish-type creature with predator-like teeth and claws.

"I'm not sure—an aquatic species of some sort."

"It must have come from that body of water out there,"

I say, hoping I'll be able to fulfill the prophecy without ever having to go for a swim in it.

"It's huge. How could the beast kill something like that?" Mark asks as if thinking out loud.

"I have a feeling that thing can kill just about anything," Sandy says.

"Yes and unfortunately, I'm pretty sure it does. This used to be one of our alien friends," Levi says, bending over, checking out a particular set of bones. "It seems even they're on the menu."

"Oh god," I hear myself say out loud, feeling totally disgusted.

Levi stands up, suddenly looking alarmed.

"What is it?" Sandy asks.

"It's Reese," he says frantically, then takes off out of the room without another word.

Slipping as we make our way across the moss-ridden floor, we follow him as he quickly makes his way back out into the forest from the safety of the cave. Before any of us are able to start running, Levi stops suddenly, then turns and yells for us to halt.

The second we do, a giant bolt of lightning suddenly strikes Levi directly in the chest, sending him flying backward as a tremendous crack reverberates all around.

"Holy shit," Mark exclaims as we all stand there dumbfounded, shocked by the enormity of what just happened.

Before I have time to rush to him or help him in any way, he's already sitting up, already sensing Reese and her own need of help.

"I have to get to her," he says worriedly, jumping up.

"Jo," Sandy says, eyeing me.

I nod, knowing exactly what he's getting at right before we all take off.

As we run through the forest behind Levi, I quickly realize we're not only headed toward the structure, we're also headed toward the beast.

Its heartbeat is thumping rapidly; I can tell it's engaged in some way. Not running, but active.

It must be Reese. That thing must have left us in the confines of the cave to go after easier prey. So did it think we'd just hang out in its den until it made it back to eat us?

The minute the giant structure materializes, I begin to hear a low, menacing growl coming from somewhere directly up ahead.

Getting closer, we continue to make our way through the forest until we see them. Chi, with her spears drawn and her back to us, is standing above Reese, who seems hurt as she lies on the ground holding her side.

As we run up to them, Chi stays fixated on a particularly dense section of the forest in front of her as Levi drops to his knees beside his sister.

Sandy eyes Chi questioningly right before we hear the cracking of tree limbs as the foliage in front of us starts to move.

Slowly, with its large powerful body hunched over on all fours, the giant beast emerges from the trees. Snarling at us with a large snout full of teeth, the kind of teeth that could easily rip someone limb from limb, it eases toward us, its claws digging into the ground with each step.

Taking a step back, I feel myself respond just as I hear Mark swear under his breath.

The moment I feel the welcoming sting on my hands, it abruptly stops moving.

With piercing black eyes, it stares at each of us with an intellectual awareness that's not only creepy but truly unsettling. It's like its sizing each of us up.

"What's the plan?" Mark asks under his breath, causing

the beast to look right at him and snarl.

Feeling the energy within me suddenly at my disposal, I concentrate, hoping that if I can actually hit this thing, it will have an effect, any effect.

As if sensing my threat, the beast looks right at me, then, lifting itself up on its hind legs, lets out a massive roar. Unlike anything I've ever heard, the sound, terrifying me to my very core, causes my body to react. I send a blast of energy, then watch as the beast easily dodges it.

Faster than I would think possible for something of that size, it lunges at me, furiously slashing me with its claws, causing searing, red-hot pain to instantly erupt throughout my body.

My thoughts, a jumbled mass of pain and disbelief, are scattered as I find myself suddenly being pulled back away from the beast, then quickly picked up.

Swiftly, Sandy and Chi maneuver themselves until they're behind the beast, trying to draw its attention away from me. Enraged, the beast snarls at them but then turns back toward me. Maybe it doesn't see them as a threat, or it's just more pissed at me because I tried to hurt it with one of my energy blasts.

Either way, it ignores them completely then rears up as if it's going to lunge at me again.

Levi, suddenly appearing from somewhere off to my side, tackles the beast just as a bolt of lightning streaks out of the sky, striking them both. Sparks fly in all directions as the force of the strike throws them both backward.

Mark gently picks me up, then, holding me with a strength I didn't realize he had, takes off running headed to the structure. Feeling a stinging numbness in my abdomen, I glance down at my bloodied shirt, seeing that's it's been torn to rags. Great, what am I going to wear now?

Arriving at the structure, Mark keeps holding me in his arms as we wait for the others.

"I'll need to stand to get through the vines."

"Are you sure you can?" he asks, an edge to his voice I've never heard before.

"Yeah, I'm healing," I say, giving him a weak smile.

Gently, he places me down in front of the vines as the others come up. Reese, seemingly still in pain, stands there holding onto her side as Levi glances at her worriedly.

"Go through first so you can help her on the other side," Sandy says to Mark, eyeing my torn, bloodied shirt with his own look of concern.

Stepping onto the vines, I try to clear my mind, all the while watching as Mark, Reese, and Levi fall through easily. After a few minutes, I finally feel the strange sensation of the foliage underneath me beginning to give way, then slowly I start to sink into the jumbled mass of ivy.

Once I'm halfway through, Sandy and Chi step on, then instantly start to sink. My god, am I the only one unable to calm my mind at a decent rate?

Closing my eyes, I try harder. It's only a second before I hear it and realize what my problem is . . . the faint heartbeat of the beast. It's alive.

Pushing the fear away, I clear my mind enough that I'm able to sink through the vines until I'm free of them. Until I fall.

11

—

"I've got you," Mark says, catching me in his arms just as Sandy lands with a thud on the stone floor beside us.

Gently, Mark sets me down. We're back in that dazzlingly blue-hued bug-lit room with the sloping floor.

"We have a problem . . . the beast is still alive," I say, trying to wrap my mind around the fact that it survived the lightning.

"It wasn't fried when I left, so I assumed it could be," Levi says as he caters to his injured sister.

"Are you healing?" Sandy asks me worriedly as he glances over at Reese.

"Yeah, I'm healing," I say, knowing he's sensing something's wrong with my ability to heal but not wanting to freak Mark out.

"Let me see," Mark says, suddenly looking worried.

Lifting what's left of my shredded, bloody shirt, he inspects what I can only assume are huge gashes in my side, without reacting in any way.

"Jo you're hurt," I hear Harrison say in my head then.

"Yeah, that beast thing clawed me," I say, surprising the others until they remember.

"Can you ask Harrison where my dad is?" Mark asks quickly, trying to be nonchalant about it, but by the look on his face telling me he's feeling otherwise.

"Harrison . . ."

"I'm finding out," Harrison says, knowing my thoughts.

I realize then not only do I seem to be taking longer to

heal than usual, I notice Reese is, too. Is it something to do with the beast, or is it some affect this planet is having on our abilities?

"Guida says it's the beast," Harrison says then. "I guess it has a toxin or something inside it that you were exposed to when it clawed you."

"That doesn't sound good."

"It's okay; she says you'll heal like normal, just a bit slower."

Just as I'm passing the message along to the others, I catch sight of movement over to our right.

Glancing over, I don't see anything other than the tunnel Sandy and I came through when we entered the room earlier.

"By the way, you may want to get back-up here. Mitchell says since the storm's stopped whatever's happening could happen any minute."

"Okay, we're on our way," I say, willing myself to try and heal faster. Mitchell may be a brute, but he knows his stuff. If he thinks something's about to happen, then there's a good chance it is.

With the pain from my wound making me feel more vulnerable than usual, my thoughts become a flurry of inse-curities swirling about in my head as we make our way across the sloped room. How am I supposed to live up to some prophecy's expectation when everything I've done to get us all here is always so reflexive, so instinctual? Never that of a true hero, with the ability to contemplate every decision, every action in such a way to come about with the best, most noble conclusion.

Even with my thoughts distracting me, I catch sight of it: a small alien head peeking from around the corner of the exit.

"Do you see that?" I say right before a little alien, almost an exact replica of the other aliens, unexpectedly runs into the room.

Coming right up to us, wearing a smaller version of the alien outfit made from the same unfamiliar material, it stops, then stands there staring at us with a look of wonderment.

Everything about this miniature alien is just like its larger counterparts with one strikingly notable exception. This cute little being, with the same apparent pleasant demeanor, is devoid the unique pattern that covers their bodies.

Watching it, I can't help but think how brave it is to be standing here in front of us, the strange visitors with ripped bloody clothes and even odder . . . individualistic personas.

"Hello there," Mark says, smiling as he drops down on a knee.

Looking right at Mark, its eyes widen with surprise.

"Oh my god, it's adorable," Reese says, drawing its attention to her.

"Your voices are the first ones she's ever heard. Their children are completely telepathic, so she can only communicate through telepathy," Harrison says.

"Harrison says she only communicates through telepathy."

"So you're a girl," Reese says to the little alien.

She smiles at Reese, then glances back as if someone said something to her. Expecting her to run off, I'm surprised when I see more little heads peek around the corner right before a dozen or so other small aliens come running into the room.

Not as brave as the one standing right in front of us, they keep themselves at more of a distance as they watch us. Seconds later, without a sound, they all, even the courageous little one, turns and runs out of the room.

Following them out, I notice they take a tunnel that's

headed in the opposite direction of us.

"I wonder where they're going," I say.

"Guida has them going somewhere safe while all this plays out," Harrison says.

"That's smart."

"Jo, this whole place—the forest, certain caves, this structure—it's all connected by a series of tunnels. It's amazing. They have this whole civilization thing going on all around us, but you'd never know."

"You're right," I say surprised by his words. "I never would have known that."

As we make our way through the tunnel to the others, I can't help but think about what Harrison said . . . about the aliens and this place. Especially about how much truly is at stake with the prophecy.

"Holy shit, what did that thing do to you?" Tom asks me as we all walk back into the tremendous room.

"Yeah, it wasn't as cuddly as you'd think," Reese says sarcastically, seemingly much better as she gives her brother a reassuring smile.

"Harrison said you'd both need new shirts, but my goodness, I wonder why it would do this to you," Ava says, inspecting my ripped shirt.

"Because it's a crazed, mindless killer," Reese says.

Ava gives her an odd look just as an alien walks over to us and hands us each a piece of clothing—a long-sleeved white shirt made from a soft, stretchy material.

"And how the hell are you still alive?" Tom asks Levi,

giving him the once-over.

"They weren't superbolts."

"Oh, well, that's good, I guess," Tom says, looking baffled. "So it really had no effect on you . . . that's crazy."

"That's one word for it," Levi says sarcastically.

Mitchell, out on the ledge with Harrison, glances up. As he begins to head toward us, three of the aliens, in their usual agreeable manner, come over, carrying similar uniquely carved wooden boxes. Having no idea what could possibly be in them, I'm shocked when in unison they open the lids, revealing the same brown, seedy, cakelike blocks in each.

"It's food . . . actually better than it looks," Tom says, reaching in one of the boxes and grabbing one.

Although I'm not feeling especially hungry, I take one anyway. It's been a while since I've eaten anything.

"I wasn't hungry, either," Tom says as he watches the others unenthusiastically reach into the boxes, each grabbing out a block. "But it did give me a little boost."

"Not sure if I like the sound of that," Reese says, biting into the soft block.

"So you did survive," Mitchell says, walking up and eyeing Levi as if seeing some cool new weapon.

"Not a scratch," Levi says as if annoyed by all the attention.

"Glad to hear it," Mitchell says, staring at him in such a way that his dark, dominating presence instantly wipes away Levi's attitude.

Absentmindedly, I bring the block of food in my hand to my lips. Although it smells earthy with hints of something toasted, I bite into the soft, chewy food and find that it actually tastes sweet.

Surprised, I look at the aliens and notice how enthralled they are by us eating their food.

"Eating for them usually has a lot of ritual involved, so they're amazed that we just grab food and eat it," Harrison says.

"Any information about those hockey-puck-looking things that fell earlier?" Sandy asks, looking at the food in his hand but not eating it.

"Most likely a diagnostic tool used to find out information about this planet before attacking it," Mitchell says, glancing toward the ledge outside.

"How much information could they possibly have transmitted before the lightning took them out?" Levi asks.

"Gregor thinks at least basic planetary schematics."

"That's not good," Levi says.

"No, it isn't. The last thing we need is for them to have more information about this planet than we do," Mitchell says.

"So what do we do now?" Tom asks just as I leave and head to the outside ledge to talk with Harrison.

"We wait for something to happen," Mitchell says.

"For what to happen?" Reese asks.

"Well, that's the million-dollar question, isn't it?" Mitchell says.

As I approach the end of the room, I notice how the sunlight reflecting off the glassy portions of the rock makes the opening seem brighter, like it's sparkling.

Walking out on the ledge, I step off to the side to quickly change my shirt. The tattered material of my old shirt feels unrecognizable as I pull it over my head. Chills course through me as I stare at the bloodied, shredded rag. If that beast did this to my shirt, what did it do to my stomach? Even though I know my wound is healed, can feel that it is, I still can't bring myself to look.

Throwing my new alien shirt on, I'm surprised that

although a tighter fit than what I'm used to, it's so comfortable that I feel like I don't even have a shirt on. A slight movement and something in the shirt sparkles in the sunlight. Looking closely at the material, I notice tiny metallic specks all throughout the soft, white fabric. That's odd.

"I think it's something to do with camouflage," Harrison says, reminding me of my surroundings.

Turning around, I see him standing on the edge of the stone ledge, facing out to the forest.

"Oh, cool," I say, finding myself feeling on edge as I walk up and stand beside him.

As we both stand here, not saying or thinking anything, we stare out, just enjoying the particular camaraderie we share in the fact that the two of us together have some special part to play in the prophecy. A fact that has irrevocably entwined our lives in a way we're still trying to understand.

"So this is really about to happen," I ask, already knowing the answer but for some reason needing him to confirm it.

"Yeah . . . it is," he says so matter-of-factly that my breath catches in my throat.

Scanning the horizon, I don't see anything, but just the thought that any minute I might agitates the energy within me.

"You know what's crazy," he says, still staring out.

"I'm not sure crazy is a word in our vocabulary anymore."

"Yeah, you're probably right," he says and chuckles.

"But do you know that with all the prophecy stuff, everything I've seen or done, do you know it's never once freaked me out?"

"From where I stand, that's a good thing."

"Maybe . . . but it just seems weird, like different from the way I used to be. Like another thing about me that's changed."

I look toward him and smile.

"You not freaking out probably has something to do with our connection and the way you're always able to calm me down. Like some ying-yang thing. You never freak out, while me . . . that's all I ever do."

"I guess that's one way to look at it," he says, smiling.

Standing there with Harrison, I study the forest and how the light streaming down from the suns casts the same shadows from the trees in exactly the same manner as before. Although a lot of time has passed, everything looks the same as it did when I was out here the last time.

"Yeah, it's weird that it's always day here," he says, reading my thoughts and reminding me how hard it must be for him to have his own original thought with me always in his head.

"How's the telepathy stuff going?"

"If I focus, I can stop the voices, or with the aliens, the sounds, but the feelings you all have attached to your thoughts . . . that's different. It's not something I seem to be able to not feel."

"After we fell earlier, did you hear or feel anything while I was out there?"

"Not really. I mean, I knew you were alive."

"You did?"

"Yeah, I can't really explain it. I couldn't hear your thoughts or anything, but I don't know . . . I just knew. So I came out here to listen for you and to be a lookout for Mitchell."

I think about Mitchell and how much he was probably freaking out.

"No, actually that was Tom," he says smiling.

The loud boom startles me, jolting my senses. Before I'm able to rack my brain for what possibly could have caused such a tremendous sound, I look up and know.

Two aircraft, foreign, ominous, come into view.

Both identical, they're small and fast. With a rounded front leading to a wide base, they each have an inconspicuous matte black hull. Something that would make seeing them almost impossible if flying in deep space or the dark side of this planet even, but luckily for us, this isn't either of those places. This is an area of a planet where the backdrop to these dark, stealthy-looking aircraft is a perpetual sunny day.

Swiftly, silently they swoop down in a perfectly symmetrical pattern. The coordinated maneuvering of these two small identical ships is seamless, perfectly executed as if the entire display was choreographed.

Plummeting fast, they're just a few yards away from crashing into land when they suddenly pull up and begin flying along the ground, headed in opposite directions. The whole thing's so flawless that I can't help but wonder how it could be accomplished without having been practiced beforehand.

Although I'm unnerved as I watch one of them head straight for us, I notice that the other ship is moving quickly in the other direction. Where is it going?

All of a sudden, noiselessly, both aircraft simultaneously stop and hover. A second later and four black cylinders rapidly lower from the bottom of each ship.

That's when I notice that people, beings, whatever, jump to the ground out of each of the tubes and take off running.

As I watch the invaders disappear into the surrounding forest, the tubes instantly lift back into each aircraft, and without so much as a pause, the ships, in unison, rapidly rise, then take off. Headed back in the direction from which they came, back to being able to blend in again, back to space.

I scan the surrounding forest, looking for the ones the spaceships left behind. Nothing.

"Scouts," Mitchell says under his breath from behind me. Everyone, all twelve of us, plus Guida and the other aliens, are now out on the ledge. I'm not surprised, considering how loud that boom was.

"Jo, two ships, eight scouts," Mitchell barks at me aggressively.

"Uh."

"Is that what you saw? That's what I saw, but your vision's better."

I barely nod before Tom, Gregor, and Mitchell begin throwing out all the different possibilities of why the scouts are here.

"There's only eight of them," Reese says, glancing at her brother as she leans against the wall, her lean, muscular body not showing any signs of being alarmed in any way. "Let's just take them out before they have a chance to get any information back to the mothership or whatever."

"I wouldn't underestimate the damage they could do. They may not just be here to get information, at least not all of them," Mitchell says, instantly changing everyone's perspective on our visitors.

"So what do we do?" Mark asks, looking gung-ho about the whole thing, obviously wanting to help out any way he can.

"We use this to our advantage," Tom says, eyeing Mitchell, challenging the strategist within him.

He smiles at Tom as if knowing exactly what he's doing and relishing it. "Exactly, we just bought ourselves some time, and when we get our hands on those scouts, some much-needed information of our own."

"They're only scouting out this side of the land mass. They must know the other side is just alien crops or whatever," Tom says.

"Information from the pods?" Levi asks.

"I'd say so. The way they came in, organized . . . planned. They knew exactly where they were going," Mitchell says.

"You think they'll come here," I ask, feeling freaked out at the thought.

"Definitely. This structure is the most likely target to gather information, sabotage us in some way—you name it."

"And the two tunnels that connect the room downstairs to the surrounding forest?" Sandy asks, eying Mitchell.

"We have to assume they know about the tunnels and where they lead," Mitchell says, knowing exactly what Sandy's getting at. "We'll need to split up. Keep this vantage point while covering that room."

"What about Guida and the aliens?" Ava asks Mitchell worriedly, glancing at the ones in the room as they stare back at her pleasantly, as if she were just talking about baking a cake. "We need to protect them."

"She's right, we have to help them," I say, thinking about those cute little alien children.

"Guida says there's no need. They're somewhere safe," Harrison says, trying to make sense of something going on in his head.

"Maybe, but I'm going to need you to figure out exactly where they are," Mitchell says to Harrison matter-of-factly. "Until then, we need to deal with our scout problem."

Harrison nods while seemingly distracted by his telepathy.

"Tom, you're with the twins, and Harrison up here . . . bird's eye view and all, plus since Harrison can communicate with Jo, it will keep you guys in the loop. Sandy, you're taking Jo and Ava down that tunnel that leads from here all the way out," Mitchell barks out hurriedly as he motions toward the exit.

"Wait . . . what! Ava isn't going with them," Tom says, looking at Mitchell like he's crazy.

"I need Ava with Jo in case we need to transport her quickly. If Jo's our weapon, I may need access to her somewhere else."

A weapon, really. One minute he puts me down, then the next I'm his special weapon.

"Chi, you Gio and Mark go through the other tunnel, out through that mating cave," Mitchell says, looking irritated for having to call it that.

Avoiding Sandy's gaze, I think about how glad I am we don't have to go through there. What would Ava think if Sandy and I started uncontrollably making out in the middle of some fight with a scout?

Harrison glances at me oddly before quickly looking away.

"Where are you going to be?" Tom asks Mitchell.

"I'm jumping down and waiting for our friends out there," he says, nodding toward the forest.

"You're what? You can't just wait out there."

"Why not? I'm more at home surrounded by trees, plus it'll give me the advantage."

"Well, I have to say, I wouldn't have thought of that," Tom says, seemingly impressed.

"That's probably why I'm here," Mitchell says matter-of-factly before telling us to get going and bring him all eight scouts, one alive but the rest dead.

12

—

Without a word, Sandy motions for us to check out the area for any unwanted visitors. Swiftly, we slip into the great hall with the sloping floor. Staying along the edge of the stone walls, we scan the entire room. With the sparkling, blue bug lights having a calming effect on my nerves, I'm easily able to adjust my vision so that even the shadowy dark corners are crystal clear.

"It's empty," we say, meeting Sandy back out in the tunnel.

"So now we split up," Sandy says, causing me to instantly feel apprehensive at the thought of being separated from Mark while hunting down some alien bad guys.

The second I feel the energy within me begin to surge, I realize this kind of emotional disruption is probably the reason why Mitchell didn't put Mark and me in the same group in the first place. He knew I'd be distracted or worse if anything happened to him.

"I'll be fine," he mouths to me, noticing my hesitation.

"I'm glad I caught you," Gregor says, suddenly appearing from the tunnel we are about to go down.

Hurriedly, he goes up to Chi while Sandy instructs the rest of us to keep watching the area.

"I'd like you to try these out if you get the opportunity," he says, holding up some metal contraption.

"See here," he says excitedly, pulling apart what looks to be three oddly shaped metal stakes all clumped together.

"I've magnetized the metal so that you can either throw

them as a unit or separately. Whichever way you choose should have the same desired effect."

Chi looks surprised when she grabs hold of the weapon.

"Yes, they're cool to the touch. You see that's the clue, which ties into the part of its properties I think you'll find the most interesting. It shrinks significantly upon coming in contact with the combination of heat and moisture."

"Heat and moisture," Gio asks as if, like the rest of us, not following what he's saying.

"You know, like the conditions you'd find inside a human body for example."

With either end of the stake coming to a sharp point while bulging out in the middle, Chi quickly understands what he's getting at. Studying the object in her hand, she pulls the three stakes apart as she tests the feel of them apart, then back together again.

"So if you stab someone, the metal should shrink, then fall out of the body, leaving nothing but a bleeding, gaping wound behind."

Chi smiles, and I'm reminded not only by the distinct severity in the sharpness of her eye teeth but by her demeanor and how lethal she is . . . weapons or not.

"Of course we don't know the anatomy of the things we're up against, so it's hard to say what effect, if any, this weapon actually will have, but no matter, we'll at least get some information," Gregor says before turning to Mark. "Be careful, son."

Nodding, Mark looks slightly uncomfortable with his dad's sudden display of affection.

"And the rest of you, too," Gregor says, glancing at me briefly.

Chi slips the new weapon in her jacket and pulls out her trusted small spears. I don't blame her. I'd want to stick with the tried and true, too, at least until I knew more about whatever those beings were that jumped from that spaceship.

"Okay, let's go," Sandy says.

Mark and I lock eyes for a moment, then leave with our perspective group.

As Sandy, Ava, and I follow Gregor back in the direction from which he came, I glance behind us but see nothing. Why does this tunnel suddenly seem so ominous?

"You're about to see portions of this structure that are quite remarkable," Gregor says, right before I notice that the tunnel splits up ahead.

"For example, their science-oriented room, although technologically unsophisticated, actually houses quite of number of unique materials."

As we pause at the fork, an alien, tall and imposing, suddenly appears from the tunnel to the right.

"Oh, hello," Gregor says pleasantly as it just stands there, watching us with a stoically keen interest.

"So that's the way out," Gregor says, pointing toward the tunnel to the left, which is also lit by the light-emitting slugs.

"But Mitchell wants Ava to come with me for a moment before you leave."

"Why?"

"I'm not telepathic, so when it comes to communication, I've been somewhat out of the loop, but I would assume it has something to do with adding this particular location into her transport abilities," Gregor says as we continue to follow him as he heads down the tunnel to the right.

"Also, I believe that alien back there is on lookout per Mitchell's request."

"That's smart," Sandy says. "If it sees anything, it would only take a thought and everyone's alerted."

Getting to the end of the short tunnel, we come upon a

narrow spiral ramp leading up into a hole in the stone ceiling.

"It looks rather unwelcoming from this perspective, but I assure you it is quite the opposite once you're up there."

Following Gregor, we all climb the steep incline, one behind the other.

"Are there aliens up here?" Ava asks.

"Yes, the majority of them are staying up here temporarily, so they're out of harm's way."

So that's where the children were headed earlier.

As we near the top, I start to see a slight pinkish hue coming from somewhere up above us.

Once at the top, we find ourselves on a small landing being bathed in the light of more glowing rocks. Following Gregor, we step through an arched entryway surrounded by an extensive display of intricate carvings in the stone and into a place I never would have imagined could exist here.

Contrasting the dark, primitive corridors that brought us here is a cluster of rooms, each one filled with groupings of aliens among an array of cream-colored plush looking furnishings and effects. While low-lying silk-covered bench-type seating abounds in the rooms, it's the silken tapestries draped over the hard, stone walls throughout that seem the most extravagant.

Guida walks up, looking like a combination of herself and Chi.

"I needed the dimensions of Chi's hands for the weapon," Gregor explains.

"They have little ones," Ava whispers to me excitedly when she notices the children standing among the adults.

"Yes, for them this is a place of learning," Guida says, causing everyone in the room to look at her with astonishment.

"Oh, it's their school," Ava says, smiling at all the aliens standing around staring at us.

"To gain that deep connection that is the school within us all," Guida says, then quickly changes back to look like her usual self just as she and every alien in the room look toward the entryway.

"What is it?" I ask, feeling unexpectedly alarmed.

Harrison's suddenly in my head: "Jo, it's one of the aliens. I don't know exactly, but something happened."

"The alien downstairs," I blurt out.

Instantly Sandy makes the connection. "They're here," he says, emotionless.

"This up here, it's yours," Sandy says quickly to Gregor, then takes off back down the spiral stairs with Ava and me right behind.

Seconds later and we're back to the fork in the tunnel, to the spot where the alien was on lookout duty, but now it is just a large, tattooed heap of bizarrely contorted limbs.

We quickly look down each of the tunnels but don't see anything.

Fear triggers my energy, sending a wave of stinging heat throughout my body.

"Tell Harrison to be on the lookout . . . uh, are you okay?" I hear Sandy ask, his voice lingering somewhere in the background beyond my abilities.

With my senses on overload, I take a deep breath, trying to calm myself and whatever the hell is making them react this way.

Thankfully it works. The second of reprieve away from my abilities and their dominance over my reasoning helps me grasp our predicament.

I swing back around and see something in the dark corner by the entryway to the spiral ramp, the same corner we all just went past.

Muscular yet lithe and agile looking, its entire body, even its head, is covered in a dark, seamless second-skin type suit.

A suit so tight that it's obvious this invader is a human, or at the very least a humanoid of some type, and that it's a male.

Ava gasps when she sees him.

Like some menacing science-fiction ninja, he's pressed against the wall, standing there watching us, watching everything. How did we walk right by him?

No one moves.

I know he doesn't come in peace—the alien dead on the ground can attest to that—but I just stand here, waiting for him to do something.

Part of me wants him to run up the ramp to the waiting mass of aliens. The same aliens that now know what he did to one of their own.

Wonder how passive they'd be now?

Slowly he starts to inch toward us. With no obvious weapons in his hands, I check out his outfit but don't see anything attached to it. No utility belt with gadgets, nothing.

"Do you speak?" Ava asks nervously.

The scout doesn't respond, not a word. Just keeps slowly coming toward us.

Sandy, looking like he's ready for whatever this guy might try, holds up his hand.

"I'd advise you to stop."

Not acknowledging him in any way, the scout continues to advance on us slowly.

"Jo, get ready to blast him."

I concentrate on my energy as I watch him come closer.

All of a sudden a blinding light that's so intense I instinctively turn away leaves me immobilized.

"Sandy, I can't see," I hear Ava say.

Blinking . . . trying to recover from the optical overload, I suddenly sense him near me. Freaked out, I begin to swing my fists all around me, hitting nothing but air. Realizing how completely vulnerable we really are, I rub my eyes vigorously in an attempt to wipe away the effects of the light.

Sandy suddenly makes a strange noise. I'm triggered. As if on cue, my ability takes over. Swiftly, I'm able to regain enough of my vision that I see the scout. Taking a strange object out of his suit, he turns and, lifting his hand to my neck, is just about to do something with it when he pauses. I've recovered and he knows it.

I grab at his hand, at the thing he has in it, but he's fast, incredibly fast. Contorting his body, he swiftly grabs my wrist, breaking it instantly as he sweeps my legs out from under me, sending me slamming back onto the hard, stone floor. Searing, white-hot pain explodes from my wrist as I lie there, shocked at having heard the crack of my bones.

Taking advantage of my debilitated mental state, the scout comes at me again with the strange metal object . . . a silver cylinder with two prongs coming off the end.

That's when I notice that each of the prongs has a jagged, sawlike edge, and my instincts take. I push at him with my good hand. I'm only able to hold him off for a second before he begins to overtake me. Just as I feel the cold metal touch my neck, he's abruptly yanked back.

Sandy, having regained his vision, throws the scout against the wall. Horrified, he pauses when he sees my hand, without the support of the bone in my wrist, flopping to the side.

The scout, having quickly collected himself from his engagement with the stone wall, stands up, then faces Sandy, his hand poised above the sleeve of his suit. A second later and a cluster of strange green symbols appear on the sleeve like some cryptic control panel.

Ava comes over to me as I awkwardly pick myself up off the ground. Her eyes having adjusted back to their usual field of vision, she looks freaked as she glances from my wound to the scout.

We all eye the scout, waiting for him to do something. To push one of those bizarre symbols and send laser blasts at us or something.

Just when I start to think his suit is malfunctioning or maybe he's bluffing, he swipes his hand in a circular motion above the panel, then drops a small disc-looking thing onto the cave floor between him and us.

Instantly a barrier appears, like some translucent energy field, from the floor to the ceiling, cutting off our access to him. Glancing back at the spiral ramp behind us, I realize somehow, through all the fighting, he's managed to trap us in the tunnel that leads up to the aliens. Smart—now he has an easy escape.

"It looks like some kind of force field," I say, holding my wrist straight as I feel it beginning to heal.

"It does," Sandy says as if contemplating whether or not he should try to touch it.

"Sandy . . . your neck," Ava exclaims.

On his neck is a place where a chunk of his flesh seems to be missing . . . like it's just been scooped out.

"Yeah, he took a piece of me."

So that's what that freak was trying to do with that creepy-looking object.

"Why would he do that?" Ava asks, looking disgusted at the scout, who's still standing on the other side of the barrier watching us.

"Probably getting samples of us to take back and study."

Sandy reaches in his pocket and pulls out the block of food from earlier.

"Stand back," he says just as I realize he's going to use the food to test the lethality of the barrier.

As soon as the scout sees he's about to throw something toward the barrier, he takes off.

"That doesn't make me feel better about this," Sandy says as he holds the block of food up.

Wincing, I hold my breath, waiting for an explosion or something. Instead the block falls to the ground on the other side of the barrier with a thud.

"It's nothing, just an illusion," he says hurriedly, then goes to pick the disc up off the ground. As soon as he touches it, the barrier disappears.

"How's your wrist?" he asks me as he slips the tiny disc into his pocket.

"Healing. I'll be fine."

"Okay," he says frowning, obviously not liking the fact that I'm hurt. "Let's hurry, but remember to expect anything."

We head in the same direction as the scout, toward the exit.

Getting to the end of the tunnel, we find ourselves going inside a small cave. Sunlight coming in through the entrance makes it easy for us to quickly look around for the scout. Nothing.

"Remember, scouts aren't the only thing we need to be worried about out there," Sandy says, causing me to absent-mindedly touch my abdomen.

Stepping out of the cave and into the sunlight, I close my eyes and concentrate. Although I can tell right away the wind has picked up, I listen to the area around us but only hear the usual woodsy sounds. Nothing that would make me think the beast is anywhere around.

"We're fine. I don't hear it, but the weather¬ . . . ," I say right before I'm struck so hard the impact of the blow sends me flying.

Landing hard against the ground, I grab at my chest while gasping for air. Panicking, I sit up, feeling my chest, my lungs, feeling everything burn while I try to force myself to breathe.

Ava falls to her knees beside me.

I can tell she's saying something, but I can't focus on her. Not when I'm fighting to breathe.

Still gasping for air, I glance over and see Sandy fighting the scout but am unable to really concentrate on what's going on.

Finally, the pain inside my chest subsides slightly, and I'm able to take the smallest of breaths. Even though it's nowhere near enough oxygen, it's at least a start.

Sandy, with the upper hand, lunges at the scout, striking him directly in the throat. As the scout steps back, seemingly stunned, I take a semblance of a normal breath and feel my body respond.

Like an instantaneous replenishment of the very essence of life, I feel vitality come back into my body as my mind at once becomes sharper.

Ava gasps suddenly, then takes off toward Sandy, who now lies motionless on the ground with the scout hovering over him.

Picking myself up, I notice the scout doesn't react at all as Ava runs toward him. He just stands there like some creepy loiterer, watching as she falls to her knees beside Sandy.

But the second he sees me standing, his perspective changes. He grabs the back of Ava's shirt, tossing her to the side as he proceeds to push some round metal object into Sandy's chest. At once Sandy's body convulses before becoming lifeless again.

With my heart in my throat, I watch as the scout then turns toward Ava.

I take off.

Reason, no longer at the forefront of my actions, is kicked to the curb as I find myself automatically drawn to Sandy as if I were tethered to him.

Within a second, I'm over him, checking for breathing, a heartbeat. There's nothing.

Looking down at him, at his face that's so strikingly handsome even now, as he lies there without a pulse, I let my abilities immediately take over my weakened mental state.

Instinctively, I place my hand on him and force my life-altering energy into him.

At once he begins to breathe again as the nauseatingly sweet taste erupts inside my mouth. Swallowing hard, I try to keep myself from vomiting as I watch life flood back into him.

Trembling, I'm left momentarily weak as relief courses through me. Then I hear her call to me.

Snapping out of it, I look at Sandy, knowing he's going to be all right, then connect back with my surroundings.

Ava's headed into the woods with the scout chasing her. I take off.

With the energy within me still stirred up, I close the gap quickly. Coming up on them, I see Ava suddenly trip and fall. The scout, missing his chance to snag her, pauses, then oddly just darts off into the forest.

A second later and I'm with Ava. Just as stunned and even more appalled.

Lying on the ground is another scout. With a huge hole where his abdomen used to be, he's on his back with all of his insides lying all around. Both of his arms, looking as though they were ripped from his body, lie far off to the side, as if tossed there absentmindedly.

I only know one thing that could have done this.

I listen for it as Ava, having tripped over one of the arms, stands up. Surprisingly, she doesn't seem freaked out at all as she looks over the scene.

"The beast did this, didn't it?"

"I would think so."

"The scout probably deserved it," she says matter-of-factly, looking around dismissively. So Ava has a little bit of a ruthless side. I smile to myself, glad to see it. A scout killed one of the aliens, so in her book, that makes him deserving of this. It makes him a bad guy, pure and simple.

"Your wrist, it's already healed!"

She's right, I think as I move it around. Other than feeling a little stiff, it's basically back to normal.

"I think it's starting to rain," she says.

Glancing up I feel a few random droplets of water wet my face but oddly no more than that.

"I hope that's all it is," I say, staring up into the sky for any indication that this could be more than just a little bit of precipitation.

"Sandy," she says all of a sudden when she sees him coming up.

She runs to him and throws her arms around his neck, while I fight to contain my emotions. He's healed and thankfully looking healthier than ever. At least that's one of my abilities I seem to have a handle on.

Sandy locks eyes with me, and I instantly, embarrassingly, tear up.

His body stiffens as he checks out the slaughtered scout.

"I know, I'm listening for it," I say when he gives me the usual look.

"Where's the other one?" Sandy asks, noticing that this scout isn't the same one he was fighting earlier.

He's right. Although not even a whole scout anymore, I can see the differences. In the suit he's wearing, his body type. So they're not alien androids built to certain specifications. All anatomically correct, all lethal.

"Grab him," Mitchell yells from somewhere in the trees

when a scout suddenly bursts out of the woods, then sprints past us.

Feeling a surge of adrenaline, I take off after him.

Different than the scout we encountered earlier, this one's fast. An obviously highly trained, naturally skilled runner, he moves through the forest easily maneuvering around the plethora of tripping hazards scattered across the ground.

Nowhere near as fleet-footed, I find myself tripping over a tree root. Stumbling forward, I catch myself before completely falling on my face but watch as the scout gets farther ahead. Aggravated, I react and instantly tap into my ability. As the energy surges within me, I take off after him again but this time close in fast.

A second later and I'm right behind him, almost able to touch him. With my lack of training and without any sense of control over my abilities, I do the only thing that comes naturally. I dive toward his back and try to stop him with a good old-fashioned tackle.

As if having sensed my proximity to him, he easily dodges my ridiculous attempt to stop him with such agility and flair that I'm pretty sure I never even had a chance of catching him in the first place. Not in such a barbaric way, anyway.

Lying on the ground, feeling much less heroic than I ever have, I feel a few drops of rain hit my face as I watch Sandy and Mitchell continue to run after him. As Ava runs by and smiles, I jump to my feet, realizing I'm going to have to start doing more than just conjuring up my energy source. I'm going to have to actually start doing something constructive with it.

13

－

Chasing the scout, we burst into a large clearing in the woods, finding ourselves in the middle of Chi, Mark, and Gio, who are fighting two other scouts. Different scouts, with similar skintight suits. I can tell right away that one of them is a female.

So this species has characteristics like us.

Instinctively I stop short, then watch as metal stakes whiz by me.

With Chi's usual accuracy, the stakes find their intended target, but the scout doesn't react, not so much as a flinch, as all three of them strike his chest then fall to the ground, leaving the scout completely and disappointingly unscathed.

What is that suit made of that flying blades can't penetrate it?

Snatching up a stake, the scout has barely a second to study it before two of Chi's discs strike him in the head, then fall like stones to the ground. Undeterred by her weapons' sudden uselessness, Chi runs at him. Seemingly just as agile, the scout swiftly jumps to the side, avoiding her strike, but not before Chi is able to retrieve her discs.

Slipping them into her jacket, she eyes the stakes. As if understanding what she wants, the scout skillfully twirls the stake in his hand before launching it at her. Like a pro, she easily adjusts to the turn of events by stepping out of the way of the lethal torpedo right before reaching out and catching it with the precision of a master knife catcher.

The scout goes after her with a series of impressive

martial arts strikes like nothing I've ever seen. Even when Sandy joins in to help fight alongside her, the scout is still a dominant force.

Spotting Mitchell, I realize that through all the chaos, he never lost sight of his intended target. He finally gets his hands on the scout we were chasing, and I watch him grab him, then, through growled obscenities and threats, lift him up by the neck then slam him back against a tree with such a force it crushes the bark underneath him.

With Mitchell's massive hand around his throat, the scout hastily gropes for something on the arm panel of his suit. Finding the intended control, his suit instantly flashes right before an electrical current begins streaming into Mitchell. Without loosening his grip on the scout's neck, he lets out a roaring yell as the voltage causes him to start shaking uncontrollably. Just as it starts to look like he can't take any more of the electrical onslaught, he breaks the scout's neck before letting go. The scout falls to the ground with a thud.

With Gio and Mark double teaming her, I watch as the female scout, smaller, more acrobatic looking than the others, touches something on the arm of her suit. Instantly a large, wide beam of light shoots out.

Everyone freezes.

The other scout, having held his own against Chi and Sandy, takes a few steps back.

"What the hell's she doing?" Mark says as she begins to sweep it over us.

Sandy seems to understand. "She's scanning us, probably downloading—"

"Grab the bitch," Mitchell yells, racing toward her.

This time when the scout touches the arm of her suit, the wide beam of light is instantly gone, replaced by small green lasers coming out of each wrist and ankle section of the suit.

"Goddamn, what now?" Mitchell says stopping short.

Gio and Mark, who are closest to her, pause when they see the strange lasers. Taking advantage of their reservations, the scout acts fast. Running right at them, she waits until she gets directly in front of them, then dives down toward them, moving swiftly between them. Gio yells out, and I watch as she and Mark go down hard, blood pouring from their ankles.

Instantly, I feel my body respond.

"Jo, he's fine," Mitchell yells at me, knowing too well that I was just triggered.

I'm sure he's thinking that with Harrison nowhere around the last thing we need is for me to kill the scouts—and everyone else.

Eyeing the rest of us as we stand, poised, seemingly ready to deal with her and her laser knives, the scout quickly taps the arm of her suit, and the deadly lasers are gone.

For a second we all hesitate, expecting something else to happen. For her to bring about yet another issue for us out of that bag of tricks she's wearing. Instead she just stands there as if contemplating her next move. What's she doing?

Ava suddenly cries out, and as soon as I see her I know. The scout wasn't unsure of what to do. She knew exactly what she was doing—she was distracting us.

Another scout, the same one from the tunnel, has somehow managed to come up behind Ava and now has her in a headlock.

All of a sudden, something in the trees activates my energy. Taking deep breaths, I try to control my body's response even as I realize something is happening all around us.

"Jo," Mitchell says, calmly yet firmly. "You need to focus. The way he has her, it would only take one movement to break her neck."

As if picking the worst possible time to make their appearance, thirty, if not more, of those cute little furry creatures suddenly appear out of the forest and begin frolicking all around us.

The three scouts watch as the little animals pleasantly scurry all around us, stopping here and there to glance briefly at Ava.

As if deeming our new visitors not a threat, the scout holding onto Ava pulls a metal cylinder out of his suit. The one with the serrated prongs used to scoop our flesh.

"No," Sandy yells as he brings it to her neck.

The second the metal digs into Ava's skin, she cries out, causing all the little animals all around us to stop and look at her.

Just as I feel the sting on my palm, the animals react.

Screeching loudly, they instantly swarm the scout holding Ava. With the speed of a thousand pissed-off ants whose anthill has been kicked in, the animals attack him.

Stumbling away from Ava, the scout fervently grabs at the animals as he tries to fight them off.

"Holy shit," I hear Mitchell exclaim under his breath.

Frantically the scout being attacked hurls the little animals to the ground, even killing a couple of them, but it's no use, they keep pouncing on him, keep biting him with such viciousness that within seconds he's thrashing around on the ground as the animals, all over him now, continue to violently attack.

My team and I just stand there, shocked, watching the scene unfold.

What can we do? The animals are everywhere—cute, furry little creatures of death all around us. Even with our abilities, we won't survive if they all of a sudden decide we're their next target.

As more of the animals flood the area from the

surrounding trees, one of the scouts tosses something high up into the air.

I watch as the object seems to hover over us for a moment, then, with a loud bang, it explodes, leaving behind a mass of black smoke.

"A signal," I hear Mitchell mutter under his breath.

"Jo, you have to help," I hear Ava yell at me, bringing my attention back to the scout still being ferociously attacked.

With the grisly spectacle playing out in front of me, it takes me a minute to grasp what Ava's getting at. That she's actually talking about me helping two little animals lying motionless on the ground in front of her.

"You have to heal them," she says, distraught now as I bend down beside her.

The animals' incessant screeching all around us has become a low, nasally growl. I look at the lump of fur lying on the ground in front of me. How am I supposed to help this animal?

Impulsively, she grabs my hand and pushes it into the soft, warm fur. Just as I'm about to think about sending my energy into the hapless creature, it ignites on its own, sending a flash of energy rushing into Ava.

As if burned by my hand, she lets go, then abruptly begins to rub her eyes.

"There's something wrong with my eyes!"

"Jo, get away from her," Sandy barks at me as some of the animals begin to notice Ava's sudden distress.

Slowly, I get to my feet.

The animals, still attacking the scout on the ground, all at once stop and, glancing over at Ava, abruptly leave him.

Then, as if on some grisly cue, I watch in horror as watery blood begins to flow freely from the hundreds of bite marks covering the scout's body. It's only seconds before he's dead, having bled out completely.

"Holy shit," Mitchell says, appalled, as if he's never seen anything like it before. As if he isn't at heart a monster that's probably done way worse to someone. Most likely someone I've held near and dear to my heart at some point.

Now feeling even more terrified of the animals frolicking all around, I watch as the two other scouts just seem to be taking it all in. Standing there in the oddly sporadic falling rain, staring.

A moment later and I realize what has their attention. It's Ava and what I now notice are the very apparent modifications to her appearance.

Ava's eyes have changed . . . morphed into the familiar amber-hued alien eyes. The eyes alter her appearance in such a way that instantly tells everyone that we now have someone else in our team of twelve considered a "special."

With the two scouts watching her intently, Ava bends down, touching, even holding a couple of the small animals while the rest of us try to figure out if we should even move.

"You didn't like that mean guy trying to hurt me, did you?" she says sweetly to the animals.

"Uh," Mitchell says, looking flabbergasted as the cute little critters playfully go all around her, allowing her to pet them; from what I can tell, they want her to. Like Ava's own personal petting zoo from hell.

Something suddenly has the hair on the back of my neck standing up. Even as I try to focus on all the little animals scampering about, I can't help but feel a familiar sense of dread activate my energy source.

Great, the last thing we need right now is to have that bloodthirsty beast-thing trying to rip us to shreds.

Before I have a chance to warn the others, all the animals, in unison, suddenly stop moving about and, sitting up on their back legs, freeze in place, as if listening to the area around us.

They must sense it, too.

A second later and they take off, bounding back into the surrounding forest from which they came.

As the last of Ava's furry friends blend back into the tree line, I listen. It's out there, I know it. I just can't seem to home in on it.

Concentrating harder, I suddenly feel the shift in movement and the subtle sound of it leaving his hand. Before my brain is able to catch up with what I somehow know was just hurled at us, Chi's there, causing the stake to change directions midair with just a motion of her hands.

She's seemingly surprised by what she just did; the stake heads away from us and out into the surrounding forest just as the scout targets the other person in our group with unique eyes.

The stake strikes Sandy, who's without the protection of the scouts' impenetrable suit. The metal stake pierces his flesh, stabbing him in his side.

With Gregor's usual penchant for design perfection, the odd weapon does exactly what it was created to do. Reacting with Sandy's warm, slick insides, it shrinks, causing it to subsequently slide out of his body, leaving a bloody, oozing hole behind.

The sight of Sandy groping at his wound to try and stop the bleeding causes my ability to respond.

Angrily, I send one of my energy bursts directly at the scout, then thoughtlessly rub the stinging sensation on my palm as I watch the scout look down at his suit then slowly at the other scout, as if confused by what I just did.

It didn't it kill him, or even knock him down. No, instead, strange symbols start flashing on the face shield, while the odd, muted color of the suit begins to phase through a multitude of variations of other muted colors. It's like my energy blast was absorbed by the suit, so now it's reacting, maybe even malfunctioning.

As I stand here watching the scouts' suit camouflaging capability continue to falter, it starts raining, a hard, heavy rain that leaves me instantly soaked and unable to see well through the densely falling wall of water.

What is it with this planet's erratic weather?

My senses are just as drenched as my clothes, and they're suddenly on us, two different scouts ambushing us as if it were some sort of choreographed attack plan.

Frozen, I'm unable to move as the mayhem unfolds before me.

Did they plan this? Could they have?

Even as I contemplate the absurd notion, I watch as Chi fights to protect Ava from one of the newer scouts as the other one swiftly attacks Sandy.

With the nerve-racking rain falling all around us, all I can do is watch the scouts, my team . . . all fighting, all asserting themselves for an agenda that I still don't understand.

Just then, Sandy, groping at something on his neck, stumbles then falls to the ground, unmoving.

The scout then turns his attention to me, but before he's able to come at me, Gio's there, knocking him back, distracting him, and giving me a chance to get to Sandy.

The second I do, I know he's alive. Not by his breathing or pulse. No, it's because he's looking right at me, even around me, but unable to move. As if he's been paralyzed.

I touch his face, wondering what they could have done to cause this. My touch causes his head to move ever so slightly, and that's when I see it. Some sort of flat, hexagonal-shaped patch stuck to the back of his neck. Is that what's causing the strange paralysis?

Reaching down, I yank it off his neck.

The change in him is instantaneous. He begins to move ever so slightly. Only minute, tiny movements, but enough to tell me the effects of the patch are already wearing off.

As I revel in this small victory, his eyes suddenly widen, and I whip around.

Coming at me with every intention to turn me into a useless heap of energy, the scout rubs his hand on the side of his suit, removing a piece of its odd material. It was so fast, so sleight-of-hand that if I hadn't been checking out the suit and its strange patchwork material, I wouldn't have noticed it.

But I did, and now with the same swiftness the scout turns away from me just long enough to come at me from a different angle. An angle that makes it easier for him to brush by me in such a way that he's able to quickly attach the object to my neck.

The second he does, a warm sensation runs down my spine right before my entire body goes numb. My feet, hands, even my lips lose all sensation. Everything, every single nerve in my body is cut off as if by an invisible switch the scout flipped.

Unable to hold myself up a second longer, I fall right beside Sandy onto the soggy ground with an unnerving splat.

As I lay there freaking out, the rain stops just as instantaneously as it started. The constant noise of persistently pelting drops hitting the ground a hundred times a second is gone, replaced with my ability to use some of my senses to their fullest again.

My senses but not my body; one replaced by another. A cruel twist in what is starting to look like a hopeless fight against these scouts.

Chi's beside me then, crouching down as she reaches out to me. Even in my incapacitated state, I'm still able to feel my energy suddenly surge the moment she touches me.

That's when I begin to feel the effects of the patch on my neck dissipating as a multitude of sensations course through my body. Even as my brain is able to accept the fact that my body is regaining its abilities, it isn't until I see Chi stand up, her eyes completely closed as she drops the patch on the ground beside me, that I realize why.

Suddenly I hear Mark yell my name, then I watch from my disturbing sideways view as he runs at me.

Completely immobilized, all I can do is just lie there, helpless, as I watch the scout speedily run up behind him. Unable to yell a warning, I watch as the scout skillfully swipes his hand over his suit, removing another of the patches.

Stealthily maneuvering himself next to Mark, he's just about to attach the patch when the scout's suddenly thrown back as if by some sort of strong air current. Like a powerful isolated gust of intense wind focused directly on him.

"Jo?" Mark asks from right beside me.

Feeling my body regaining its mobility again, I'm able to lift my head and look at him, then shakily, but quicker than I would think possible, I sit up.

"Mark," Sandy suddenly yells from the other side of me.

Before Mark has a chance to even turn around, the scout's there. The female, the one with green knife-like lasers now jetting out from her wrists.

She slices at him as she sweeps by. Two distinct movements of her arms executed with extraordinary precision.

My breath catches in my throat as my mind gropes for a way to accept what I just saw. Even as I know he was hurt, see the red slowly soaking the side of his shirt, I still hold out hope that it was just some feeble attempt to distract us again, to keep our thoughts just as chaotic as the scene all around us.

It's when he winces as he grabs onto his side that I know

what's happening. We're losing, and the scouts, the supposed preliminary fight in this prophecy, are winning.

Quickly I scan the area, finding my confirmation.

Mitchell, his body covered in bloody gashes, curses at two of the scouts while Gio lies motionless at his feet.

Sandy, his movements still seemingly odd, uncoordinated, heads over to help Mitchell and Gio, just as Chi's knocked back.

I look at Mark. If I don't do something now, all is lost. Not just those of us in this clearing fighting this particular fight, but everyone. Everyone fighting, everyone we're supposed to be fighting for. All lost.

"Mark," I say under my breath as my feelings spur my actions.

Weakened but able to move easier now, I put my hand on Mark, then quickly try to focus my thoughts on pushing my energy into him, on healing him.

The moment I do, I begin to feel the restricting effects of whatever was on the scout's patch start to dissipate faster. Slamming my eyes shut, I push harder, hoping that if I can just get myself back to normal . . .

Ava suddenly screams, and I instantly lose my focus. I can't help it. Not when every cell in my body recognizes what's happening before I even realize it.

I look over at Ava, now down on the ground with a scout standing above her. I freeze, unable to move, to yell out, to do anything. I realize the only thing that could freak me out this much isn't just coming right at us but is already here.

Before I can even look in the direction of its snarling growl, the beast, with its large, monstrous body, bursts through the trees then in one lethal, ferocious leap, grabs the scout standing over Ava in its jaws, and is gone again, back into the trees, back into the area surrounding us.

No one moves or makes a sound as we all, even the scouts, try to wrap our heads around what just happened. It isn't until we hear the scout screaming somewhere off in the distance that we snap out of it. Instantly focus back to our surroundings.

I can tell I'm normal. Like the last of the patch's effects on my mobility was counteracted by what I just witnessed, by what I'm still trying to shake as I glance around at the others.

Just as I feel as though something else is about to happen, it does. With a changed perspective only the beast could bring upon so quickly, the scouts react.

14

—

As if hoping to regroup or possibly just put more forest between them and the beast, the scouts quickly change their tactics.

In a characteristically coordinated attempt to retreat, the scouts simultaneously attack those of us that seem least affected by their earlier assaults.

With my nerves still rattled, I see the scout come at me but am unable to respond. Just as I feel my body buckle from the force of his kick, it streaks by me. A perfectly thrown stake impales his body, penetrating the malfunctioning suit.

Chi, her eyes having morphed the moment she claimed her newfound ability to bend the air around her, helps me up just as another scout passes by. Before I'm able to figure out what he did, Chi's down, a result of dividing her attention at such a critical time.

Reaching down, I rip the patch off of her, then scan the area, looking for him, knowing at any minute he could dash by me and leave me just as debilitated.

That's when I see Mitchell step directly in the path of the laser-knives-wielding female scout.

"Where do you think you're going?" he says, grabbing her by her neck then lifting her up even as she continues to hack away at him.

Exhibiting the kind of formidability brought on by his usual brutal nature, he sneers at her even as his clothes become more bloodied by the minute. Just as I start to wonder if he's even able to feel her knives as they penetrate his skin, she lands a deep stab to his shoulder.

As if more pissed than hurt, he growls at her before tossing her back hard against a tree.

That's when I see him, the scout with the debilitating patches. He rushes at Mitchell in some veiled attempt to help his comrade but at the last minute turns toward me. I brace myself, knowing what he's going to attempt. Realizing if I try to avoid him and his paralyzing weapon, he'll get me easily.

Taking a step back as he runs at me, I feel the energy within me react, then quickly notice it's not just an internal change.

For a split second, I replay in my mind the effects my energy had on the other scout's suit, how it seemed to take away some, if not most, of his dominance over us. Hoping for the same outcome but somewhere deep down knowing better, I watch as the scout easily dodges my usual answer to being attacked but a second later, surprisingly, stops coming at me altogether.

Something in him has switched. Standing there, he just looks my way, then, as if with some sort of new agenda, takes off headed for the trees. Without hesitating, I follow. I can't let him get away.

Chasing behind him, I match every turn, every minuscule adjustment exactly, as we make our ways through the woods. I'm trying to gain ground on him, but even though I'm maneuvering through the trees just like him, like a pro, I can't. He's like the other scouts, not only fast, but fleet-footed, almost weightless. Like it's a prerequisite to becoming one of these assholes.

I push myself harder, feeling my energy within giving me just the boost I need until I'm finally right behind him.

Just as I'm about to reach out and attempt to grab him, he raises his arm and shoots an array of tiny metal objects into the air.

An instant later and each of them light up, then begin flying all around us like annoying little mini-drones.

Distracted by the harm these latest gadgets could inflict, I slow up, then watch, shocked, as a second later there isn't just one scout trying to get away from me but about twenty. Exact replicas of the scout I'm chasing.

Twenty or so of the same scout running in a multitude of directions away from me.

Pausing, I try to figure out how the mini-drones are managing such an optical illusion and which scout is the actual one I need to follow.

My hesitation gives him just the opening he needs. He's suddenly behind me, tapping me on the shoulder. I swing around just as his fist slams directly into my face.

Stunned, I fall backward onto the ground, suddenly realizing there's more to this guy than his patches.

With my entire face having erupted into a stinging throb, I barely have time to acknowledge he's not done with me before I feel the full impact of his foot hitting the side of my head.

Struck hard, my head slams to the ground. I lie there on my side, stunned by the brutality of the strike. The taste of blood fills my mouth.

I hear the hit, even discern the crack of bones, but feel nothing. Sitting up, I stare, shocked as I realize why. The bones weren't mine.

Another scout, more muscular yet just as agile looking, has appeared and is fighting the other scout.

Getting to my feet, I spit blood from my mouth as I watch the newer scout exchange blows so vicious, so strangely specific that the other scout just stands there for a moment before sinking to the ground in a motionless heap.

Without even a moment of hesitation, he bends down and, grabbing the arm of the scout, turns it in such a way that a panel on the forearm lights up. Without even glancing my way, he proceeds to push a series of buttons. The suit seems to come alive. Lights flash all over it. Different lights flickering in a persistently urgent manor.

I'm so focused on the spectacle before me it takes me a minute to realize that the newer scout has stepped back, away from the other one.

Why? What's about to happen?

Instinctively the energy stirs within me.

I notice then that the wind is starting to pick up.

With my hair beginning to whip about around my head, I suddenly hear it, a familiar hissing noise coming from the scout's suit. It can't be. The last time I heard this noise was when the pods lying all over the ground spontaneously disintegrated.

The scout's suit goes dark. He doesn't react, not even a flinch, as the suit begins to move—a strange, fluid wriggling movement.

Repulsed, I turn away the moment the pungent smell hits me. Even with the air churning all around us, I can smell it. Like a mix between the sour aroma of acid from science lab and that undeniable whiff of rot I used to smell every time I'd run by the house where that huge orange tabby cat lived. Where the undeniable stench from the decomposing carcass of its latest kill permeated the area.

On edge as I try to wrap my mind around why the scout just committed such an atrocity to one of his own, my breath catches in my throat when he turns and looks my way.

Before I'm able to react, to even think about what to do against a being like this, he reaches up and snatches off his skintight helmet.

Stunned, all I can do is stare.

With a head full of unruly red hair and strikingly chiseled features, he's, for all intents and purposes, just a man.

A man that's special. Special like me, like everyone else with eyes like me, everyone with abilities that manifest the energy differently, remarkably.

"You're like us," I murmur.

With the all-too-familiar alien eyes, he stares back intensely, as if sizing me up.

"No," he says, then takes a moment to think before saying, "and yes."

The wind suddenly gusts.

"You are the one called Jo?" he asks in an arresting manner of speaking.

"What?" I mutter.

"You are Jo?" he asks as the wind gusts again.

"Uh, yes, but how is it you speak English . . . that you're human? That you know me?"

He smiles then. A weird smile, as if he can't believe what I just asked.

"She knew I would be asked that."

"She?" I ask, noticing him looking serious as a light on his forearm flickers briefly. Before I have a chance to ask him about it, he quickly puts his helmet back on.

I don't know if it's the wind or the fact that my abilities are connected to my emotions, even my instincts, but the second he covers his head and is back to looking like that ruthlessly horrifying scout, I feel the energy within me stir.

Just as I begin backing away from him, wondering if I'm onto something, he takes his helmet off again and turns to me.

"You must trust me," he says more forcefully than I like.

"Trust you?"

Is he out of his mind? There's no way I'd trust a scout, even one that just killed another one to protect me.

As if reading me, he grabs the sleeve of his suit and rips it open, exposing his forearm.

There, branded on the smooth, muscular surface of his skin is a symbol . . . my symbol.

"It's my symbol . . ."

"Do you trust me?"

Tearing my eyes away from the brand, from the acknowledgment that this person must be connected to me somehow, I look at him, at the severity of his stare.

"Yes," I hear myself saying, as if not being able to help myself.

He smiles slightly before getting serious again.

"Then we must go to the others if you want them to live."

"Wait, what do you mean?" I ask urgently, snapping out of my indecision.

Another strong gust of wind blows. Ignoring my question, he hurriedly slides the skintight helmet back on, then motions for me to follow.

As I follow him through the woods, I try to wrap my mind around what I'm doing. That I'm running behind a scout on the way to save my friends? It seems crazy, unbelievable even, but he had the symbol on his arm. That has to mean something.

He suddenly stops running and begins looking around like he's sweeping the area.

"Do you see them?"

Without a word, a nod, anything, he takes off.

Instinctively I follow, knowing something must be terribly wrong.

Seconds later and we find them. Right before I'm able

to burst into view from the trees, the scout reaches out and stops me.

Chi and Mitchell are lying on the ground, blood splattered all over their clothes as they both struggle to get up, to heal. The female scout stands there, just a few feet away, staring down Ava.

I can't help but picture one of those old Westerns where the gunslingers meet at noon and stand in the middle of some road just eyeing each other, waiting for something to happen before they draw their guns.

This time it only takes me a second of concentration to realize what's going on. What's giving the scout pause and Ava the wherewithal to just stand there staring her down.

Even with the wind blowing through the trees all around us I still hear it, the rumbling low growl of the beast.

Although still hidden in the tree line, the female scout must know it's there. She has to, otherwise she would have already attacked.

The second Sandy, Mark, and Gio come running into the area, the beast strikes. Snarling, it lunges at the female scout, quickly knocking her to the ground.

As it eyes the rest of us, the scout quickly gets to her feet.

Seeing her standing once more, the massive animal comes at her yet again. Ready for it this time, she aims her arm at it, ejecting what looks like an array of tiny pellets.

The scout next to me takes off just as the beast is hit by the onslaught. As the beast stumbles back, seemingly more stunned by the bombardment than hurt, the male scout runs up to the female and knocks her to the ground.

Mark's next to me then as I notice that oddly the female scout isn't retaliating. No, she just sits there looking up at the other scout as he hovers over her, like they're communicating in some way.

Interjecting itself yet again into our conflict, the wind swirls around us, causing the beast to react. Shaking off the small wounds scattered across its body, it comes up on its hind legs, then, looking in the direction of the scout, roars . . . a bloodcurdling, horrific roar that reverberates through me like a shockwave.

Before anyone can react, the beast is on them, knocking the male scout back while stepping on then pinning the female to the ground under the weight of its massive paw.

My breath catches in my throat as I watch it eye the rest of us.

Suddenly Ava's there, stepping forward.

"It's okay," she says sweetly, as the wind, having settled, blows her hair gently around her head.

Fixated, it stares at her as she slowly walks toward it. Looking at her intently, it shifts his weight, causing the scout pinned underneath it to dig her gloved fingers into the soggy ground as her bones crack from the pressure.

Without a hint of fear, Ava reaches her hand out to the giant monster as if it were nothing more than someone's frightened little poodle.

No one moves. Obviously this thing has some sort of connection with her, but to what extent?

With the wind barely blowing now, we're able to hear a sudden rustling in the woods off to the right. That's all it takes to transform the settled demeanor of the untamed animal. It attacks the scout underneath it, snapping her neck, killing her with one gruesomely dominant act.

Releasing its hold on her, it looks up at the rest of us, a mix of saliva and blood dripping from its massive snout.

No one moves or does anything that could trigger it to retaliate. Not when it hovers over the lifeless body of the last thing that did.

"Well, that takes care of her," Ava says so apathetically it's shocking. "Go ahead, take her, she's yours."

As if understanding her, the beast snatches the scout up in its jaws, then stands there staring at Ava, as if connecting with her on some level that the rest of us can't even see.

Then, just as quickly as their connection began, it's severed by some random noise. Quickly the beast glances at the rest of us, then, still gripping the scout in its mouth as if she weighs nothing, bounds off toward the trees.

"Wait," Ava yells right before it disappears into the forest.

Remarkably, it does. It stops, but only long enough to stare at her for one more moment as if contemplating her, possibly even considering her safety. Can a creature like that even do that?

"Don't go far," I hear Ava say quietly, almost sadly, as if feeling some sense of loss that the beast is leaving in the first place.

Then it's gone, back into the woods, back to watching Ava with an ever-protective eye while stalking the rest of us.

Terrified at the thought that the beast could come back any minute, I listen as its heartbeat, like the steady rhythmic beat of a distant drum, validates my fear. It isn't leaving. It's doing exactly what she said. It's just lingering in the trees off to the side of us.

Distracted, I forget the others until I realize Mark's right beside me, until I hear Chi's discs leave her hand.

Hitting the male scout directly in the head, the discs fall to the ground unable to penetrate the suit. For just a split second, I'm surprised that Chi would try that again knowing it wouldn't work, but then I realize——it was just a distraction.

Chi and Sandy come at him with an adeptness that's shocking.

Before I'm able to stop them, Chi uses her evolved air power to blow him back, right into Mitchell's hands.

"No! Don't," I yell just as Mitchell grabs him by the throat.

Ignoring me, Mitchell slams him to the ground.

Unable to think, I just react, sending a blast of energy just above his head.

Everyone freezes, then looks at me as if unsure what to think.

"He's here to help us."

Mitchell, hesitating for a moment, lets him go, then slowly, apprehensively, the scout gets to his feet. Stepping away from Mitchell, he raises his hands as though gesturing no sudden movements, then slowly takes his helmet off.

"Your eyes . . . you're one of us," Ava says surprised.

"Whatever these assholes are, by my calculation he's the last one," Mitchell says, eyeing him strangely.

"It's because of him that he's the last," I say, not trusting Mitchell and that look he's giving him.

The scout stares back as if sizing him up. Probably trying to gauge whether he can trust him or not. It wouldn't be surprising since he just had his hand around his throat.

"I am not the last," the scout says, surprising the others.

"You speak English?" Ava asks, exhibiting a newfound sense of self-confidence.

Of course, having a killer beast as your personal body guard helps.

"That's good, it'll make it easier for me to sort through your bullshit," Mitchell says, his hands folded across his chest as he stares daggers at him.

The scout glares at him for a moment, bristling at Mitchell's attitude.

"There are others coming," Sandy asks.

"Many, but only one of significance . . . the one you would call the general."

"The general . . . are you kidding? Do you know how ridiculous that sounds?"

"What do you mean by what we would call?"

"Since I speak your language, know things of your cultures, it seems that is the best way for you to think of him."

"Okay, well if you're here to help, how do we stop this general guy?"

"You can't. Jo has not come into her powers yet," he says, looking at me oddly. "Which means none of you have."

"How do you know she hasn't come into her powers?" Mark asks, clearly not liking that this guy knows something about me.

The scout eyes him for a second, then looks away, ignoring his inquiry. It seems the scout either doesn't like Mark or didn't like the question. Either way, Mitchell seems to be the one most perturbed by the exchange.

"Jo is not ready, so when the general gets here, he will either capture or kill you," he says, so matter-of-factly that for a minute I wonder if he's kidding.

"What?" Mark says. "Are you out of your mind? There has to be a way to take him out."

Irritated, he looks at Mark, then the rest of us.

"Yes, there is a way. That's why I am here. I can stop him."

"You," Mitchell says, as if he's not buying it.

"Of course," he says, as if surprised that Mitchell doubts him.

"This general guy, he must be the man from Guida's cave drawing," Gio says, drawing the scout's attention particularly.

"The one with that guy standing among the corpses," Mark says.

"You have all seen this likeness of him?" the scout asks, his interest piqued all of a sudden.

"It's drawn on one of these cave walls."

"So there is a seer here?"

"How do you know about seers?"

He seems confused by the question.

"To know a seer is to know all."

"To know all," Mitchell asks, obviously wanting this guy to tell us what he knows.

"Is that the 'she' you spoke of earlier?" I ask, my mind starting to make the connections.

"Yes. I have always had a seer. She has been guiding and teaching me my entire life. She is how I know of you, your language, your planet."

"The prophecy?"

"Of course, that is how everyone knows of it, through the seers. There are only two known seers, but I have heard there may be another. Possibly it's the one from this planet," he says, stopping to contemplate it for a second.

I think of Harrison. Of how Guida said he would become one of these seer people.

"Our knowledge of the prophecy is what has brought me here, what is bringing the general here."

"Another vague bit of information to go off of," Mitchell says.

"What have you heard of the prophecy?"

"That you, Jo . . . ," he says, looking directly at me, "with the help of others could change my world. You could help turn my world into a place in which all those with or without powers can all to live together—freely, without rule."

My heart sinks. Again with me changing things.

"Your planet is governed by a ruler?" Sandy asks.

"Of course, like your own."

"Uh, what?" Mark says. looking at him as if he's not following.

"There are those on my planet who believe the authority of the ruler to be unjust. That those who can harness the energy are not superior in any way to those who do not."

"You are one of those people? Who thinks your ruler is unjust?"

Ignoring the question, he goes on. "So you see, the ruler of my world, he will not stop until you and the others are no longer a threat to him, to his rule."

"So that is why you are going to help us."

"Yes, because I believe that when change is needed, it is just. So I am here to help you find your rightful place in the cause and in my world."

15

—

"WHAT'S YOUR PLAN FOR TAKING THIS general out?" Mitchell asks.

"I have dealt with him before. He will not resist me once he realizes who I am."

"Is it because of your eyes, because of your special abilities?" I say, wondering how connected he truly is with us.

He seems confused by the question and ignores it.

Turning to Ava, he asks, "I saw you have a connection with that beast. Can you control it?"

"I think I can."

"Ava, I wouldn't be so sure," Sandy says. "Granted, it seems to want to protect you, but that's a lot different than you being able to control it."

"I know, but you don't understand. I knew what it was thinking. I mean, I knew that it didn't want to upset me."

"Yeah, but Ava . . ."

"You knew its thoughts?" I ask, unable to wrap my mind around trying to process the thoughts of a thing like that.

"In a way. I mean, I knew what it was thinking because I could feel its feelings. It was basically the same thing. Like I knew that it was angry . . . no, more like furious, but not at me . . . just at the rest of you."

"Great, your pet werewolf was furious at me. That's not disturbing," Mitchell says.

"It's not a werewolf."

"Ava," Sandy says, as if trying to talk some sense into her, "whatever it is, it still doesn't seem like the kind of thing that would be that controllable."

"What if it is?" Gio chimes in. "At least for her. You saw

how those furry little killers were with her, and now . . . this thing. Come on, Sandy, you know it's tied to her abilities."

"Sure, but this ability, it could kill her if she isn't careful."

Jarring my senses, a resounding boom suddenly reverberates all around us.

Looking up, I see them come into view. Spaceships, just as dark and ominous as the ones that dropped the scouts earlier with one unnerving difference . . . there are a lot more of them.

Quickly they descend from the sky, then fan out in such a way that I can only assume they must be familiarizing themselves with the terrain.

"We need to get to the structure," Mitchell yells.

"Wait, we can finish this quickly if I have your help," the scout says, looking surprisingly impassive in the midst of such a display.

Mitchell and Sandy glance at each other. They're not buying it, but what choice do we have? If this scout can truly help us, then that's our best shot.

As the ships sweep the area in formation, another ship comes into view. Larger but with the same angular shape and black hull as the others, it descends slowly toward the ground until it gets to a certain height, then stops.

Exhibiting a commanding presence, it just sits there, hovering over us as the other ships scattered throughout the area suddenly swoop down before stopping just a few feet from the ground.

As I feel the energy within me stir, the twins, with Tom and Harrison right behind, are suddenly there, breaking through the tree line as they run into the clearing, looking completely freaked.

Harrison doesn't say a word, not even inside my head, as he looks at me as if he just saw a ghost or, more likely for him, a vision.

My heart sinks at his silence.

Hearing a simultaneous shift within the ships hovering all around us, I glance up and am met with a scene that's reminiscent of what we witnessed earlier. Cylinders dropping from the bottom of each ship, allowing a foreign invader to slip into the surrounding forest, blending easily into its backdrop.

"Jo, you better hope your friend holds up his end of the bargain, or you're about to have to start earning your keep," Mitchell says gruffly.

As the ships maneuver back around the larger ship, it begins to slowly descend to the ground. With my nerves on edge and the energy within me activated, I glance over at the scout. Stone-faced, he just stands there watching it all unfold.

Even as the smaller ships, now with three rows of green lights illuminated, begin to sound as if they are gearing up for something, he doesn't respond.

"If he can't stop this, we're going to have to fight," Sandy says. coming up to me and Mark.

"Then we'll fight," Mark says, sounding much more confident than I feel.

"Jo," Sandy says a tone in his voice that instantly causes Mark to look at me.

I don't say anything, not a word of reassurance, as I watch the large ship land on the ground a few yards away from us.

"Jo," Mark says gently as he turns me to face him.

My breath catches as I stare at him. I realize I'm not ready for a fight like this.

"I can't protect you," I say, feeling tears sting my eyes at the thought of what that could mean. "I can't protect any of you."

"You can," the scout says loudly as he comes up to me.

Even with some alien spaceship hatch lowering behind him, he just watches me, my reaction to the thought of something happening to Mark, to the others.

Then, with a smile, not a reassuring smile but a smile of triumph, he turns and faces the ship, faces what I now see coming out of it . . . the same frightening-looking figure from Guida's wall carving.

There are no corpses, no severed limbs strewn about, and yet just watching this giant as he disembarks from his ship stops me cold.

At least seven feet tall and in full body armor, it's him, the general.

Completely bald, he not only has a strange, patterned tattoo covering his face but a deep penetrating scar across his head and neck. Like his skin was chiseled away by a madman with a large knife.

My breath catches in my throat the moment he looks my way. He has the eyes, like mine, like all of us connected to the original planet. The ones called 'specials.'

Unable to move, to think, I stand frozen in place as he lumbers toward me, his massive, muscular frame wielding some sort of long-handled weapon.

"We're surrounded," I hear Mitchell say, unbelievably still able to size up the situation even as this monster closes in.

The sting on my palms resuscitates me just in time.

As the general comes closer with what I now notice is an army right behind him, the scout suddenly steps forward and holds his hand up. Instantly the entire army stops and in unison falls on bended knee, heads bowed.

It's at that moment that everything changes. I realize I've been tricked.

"Is this a good time to say it?" Mitchell says to me,

surprisingly not reacting to any of this at all.

"You're the ruler," I say to the scout, connecting the dots faster than he expected by the look on his face.

"Yes, and you're the—how do they describe you in the prophecy?—the chosen one," he says, looking disgusted by the words.

Addressing the general, he points at Ava. "She has a connection to a beast. When it comes, kill it."

"No," Ava yells, looking around as if panicked by the thought that her new friend could be hurt.

The scout, as if bemused by Ava's display, mutters something in a strange language to the general, then smiles.

Strangely the general doesn't respond for a moment, just stands there as if contemplating the scout's words. But then out of nowhere he laughs a larger-than-life, harsh-sounding laugh before responding with a deep, guttural voice in a language like nothing I've ever heard before.

"What do you want?" Tom says eyeing the scout as he steps forward.

The scout looks at him, then at Harrison and the twins, as if wondering who they all are.

"You are the seer?"

"What?" Tom says, looking at Mitchell as if confused.

"It's not him," Mitchell says, stepping forward carefully, clearly concerned about this movement being perceived as aggressive.

The scout says something in that other language to the general, then nods toward Mark.

Instantly the general responds. Motioning to two of his cronies, they react and move toward Mitchell and Mark.

Before I'm able to think, I retaliate to the threat immediately by sending a blast of energy directly at them.

It works. The scout yells for them to stop, then turns

toward me.

"So you haven't evolved. I threaten the one you seem to value the most, and yet you still do nothing. I came here to find out for myself what powers you have, what powers they have, what weaknesses. I was listening through the helmets as my 'scouts' as you call them, told me everything they saw, what they heard."

"Exactly what I thought—you were just gathering information," Mitchell says.

"Yes, by the time I came to Jo, I knew she wasn't a threat, not yet."

"Not yet's the key," Tom says, his intuition having already caught him up enough to realize this guy's not only bad but in charge.

The scout laughs. "Your right, and that's why I'm going to give you a chance to come with me," he says, looking right at me. "To come, to train, then one day once you have proved yourself worthy to rule, you'll lead beside me, with me."

"What?" I'm stunned.

"It is said you are to come to my planet and change things . . . to alter my rule, and you will, by joining me. You see, you and I, we are similar—I would say one and the same."

"You're crazy," Tom says.

"You just figuring that out now," Mitchell says snidely.

The scout bristles, then before anyone knows what happening, he blasts Mitchell and Tom with a blast of energy. Energy like mine, but stronger, more effective and, I realize as I watch them both lying on the ground, unmoving, lethal.

The action spurs the general to react. Gruffly he yells something in a foreign language as I move toward Mitchell.

Dropping down on my knees, I quickly push my healing energy into him as everything begins happening all around me.

As the foul taste erupts within my mouth, I'm hit from behind with something so powerful, so all-encompassing that it sends what feels like a bolt of electricity flowing through my body, stunning any and all of my functioning.

Falling to my side, I feel the energy course through me as I watch everything I feared could happen coming to fruition.

Everyone I rely on, love, is being attacked. With some instinctive impulse, I will myself not to heal, but to absorb the energy so unwillingly interjected into my body.

It works. I quickly feel myself return to normal.

I'm just about to get to my feet when I hear it coming . . . coming fast.

I stand up just in time to watch the beast burst through the trees, then make a beeline for the unfortunate members of the ruler's army who happen to be around Ava.

Although they're well armored, the beast is strong, unnervingly brutal, and insanely angry. As if adrenaline instead of blood is flowing through its body, it tears into the attackers, killing many of them before being brought down by a blast of the ruler's energy.

I watch as it falls to the ground, the weight of its body crushing another hapless victim.

It's Ava's reaction that ignites the ability within me, causing me to thoughtlessly send a burst into its massive, lifeless body. Even as my brain tells me it didn't need a mercy kill, my body rejects the notion, even as it fights back my sudden urge to vomit.

"You see, I will get my way," I hear him say from behind me.

Spinning around, I'm instantly locked in his gaze. An odd, cold gaze that sends a chill through me.

"Like I told you before, I'm here to help you."

"Help me?" I mutter, unable to wrap my head around

this crazy person's line of thinking.

"Yes," he says as I watch every member of my team fall victim to the attackers. "Help all of you find your rightful place in my world."

Epilogue

—

The steady, continuous vibration of the ship dulls my thoughts. Even as random flashes of Tom lying motionless on the ground infiltrate my consciousness, I examine its massive frame, continuously studying the beast's distinctive characteristics, the ones that made it so formidable, so perfectly deadly. Those same attributes I can't seem to tear my eyes away from now.

I study its massive claws, each one signifying the creature's complete dominance, its brutality. I study its large, powerful jaws, the very essence of what's needed to bring about death in a horribly violent way.

How can I not be moved by the loss of such a specimen? One so terrifying yet so connected to Ava, to us.

Even now, as I sit here Ava's muffled sobs pervade my conscience, thankfully confusing my ability to connect my feelings to an appropriate catalyst, to Tom, to our predicament . . . to anything else residing within the depths of my subconscious. The one place I dare not go. Not when my control over my abilities is so limited.

The ship leans to the left, instantly breaking my mind's incessant ponderings.

With my attention inconveniently brought back to my surroundings, I lock eyes with Sandy but find, since I was momentarily disconnected from reality, I can't understand the meaning he's so obviously trying to express.

Looking past the passengers to the structural makeup of this spaceship, I'm astounded at its functionality.

With the practicality of every military plane I've ever seen on TV guiding my expectations of how an alien space-ship would really look on the inside, I glance around feeling surprisingly satisfied. I guess there's no substitution for the utilitarian nature of hard, gray metal surfaces when it comes to the transport of unexpectedly varied cargo or, in our case, prisoners.

Feeling a shift in the ship's mechanisms, I glance around at the ones chosen to fly on the same contraption with me.

With Chi and Sandy showing interest in what's happening on the outside of the ship now, Harrison, with his arm around Ava, acknowledges my switch in perception.

It's the change in perspective that draws my attention to the large panel window right behind Harrison. Since leaving Guida's planet, there's been nothing to see but the black abyss of space, but now, since altering course, there's something else. A planet.

A planet that through my high school science-class knowledge of the cosmos seems to have all the colors needed to sustain life.

With my attention diverted from the beast as I watch our destination through the window grow larger by the minute, I inadvertently fail to connect the recognizable sound of its life force activate until its heart rate, having become a steady strong beat, suddenly ignites the energy within me.

Looking around at the others, at the inside of this metal ship, I find myself surging as I try to grapple with the inevitable. At the fact that in mere seconds this beast is not only going to be conscience but exhibiting its usual temperament . . . pissed.

The instant I say her name, it opens its eyes. That's the instant I know. If we're going to survive this, the beast, this prophecy, than I'm going to need to step up . . . to evolve.

So I do.

Book 4 of *The Altered Elite* series coming soon!

Discover more books at

dburgardbooks.com

www.ingramcontent.com/pod-product-compliance
Lightning Source LLC
Chambersburg PA
CBHW020520120726
47904CB00003B/908